MW01125407

Rachel's Journey

MERRI GAMMAGE

Copyright © 2019 Merri Gammage

Published by Merri Gammage
merrigam@yahoo.com

Edited by JoEllen Claypool
Cover Photo by Tina Phillips and Merri Gammage. All rights reserved.
Cover Designed by Merri Gammage, Tayler Gammage and JoEllen Claypool. All rights reserved.

Printed in the United States of America
February 2019

ISBN: 9781796824735

LCCN: 2019904272

Book #1
The Throne of Brimley Series

Rachel's Journey

MERRI GAMMAGE

CONTENTS

DEDICATION

Thank You, God, for the desire to write. Thank you to my family, for the inspiration to write. Thank you to my friends, for reading what I write.

Eagle Island

★ = Begin/Return
----- = Rachel's Route
|———| = 30 Miles

TRAVEL DAY ONE

She thought she might love him, eventually, but as she watched him sleep, she gathered her things, left a note by his bed, and headed out with little regret. The morning air was cool and smelled of crisp, mountain pines. Spring brought little change to her small village, tucked at the base of the Conner Mountains. The city of Brimley was divided into regions; Rachel lived in the most rural, Brimley Downs. For as long as she could remember, her home had been in this colder region. She checked the sky – probably another two hours before dawn and she would have a long journey in front of her. Rachel was nineteen years old, only months away from twenty, and on her way to the forbidden elven village of Geerda to get help for her little brother, Jon.

Jon was only six and Rachel cherished him. She had believed they were of the same flesh and blood until nearly eight months ago when he became very ill. The local doctors had tried various cures with no luck and the family's blood had been tested to aid in the process, but Rachel's was not a match. It was then that she learned the truth about being taken in by the Mills as a toddler.

Jack and Mavis Mills were all Rachel could remember for parents. They were always loving and fair, but lately, she had not been on the best of terms with them. They wanted her to move closer to the palace in Brimley Heights for trade school the past autumn – away from everything she knew. She hadn't even decided what she would do for a living yet.

Jack was a farmer and rancher of sheep and Mavis a wool spinner. They made a comfortable living, even in these tougher times, but like most parents, they wanted more for Rachel. They were frustrated with her lack of drive. Rachel, however, had always felt there was something missing, some unknown future that would eventually just present itself.

With the tension of dealing with Jon's illness and the constant arguing with her parents, it was just too much. She had moved in with her boyfriend, Lane, three months after her nineteenth birthday.

This was one more thing to add to the strain of their relationship.

Lane was a friend Rachel had met the last year of school. When he and Rachel were together, she felt content, she felt happy, she felt comfortable. Lane was safe. Rachel knew he wanted more from her, for her to return his feelings, but he would never pressure her. His desire was for Rachel to realize in her own time that he could make a future for them. She had only been officially dating him for about seven months. He was there for her when Jon first became ill, and they shared a tender kiss, but nothing beyond that. Life was just rolling along for Rachel; she didn't see any reason to go looking for someone else. Plain and simple – she settled.

Rachel explained in her note to Lane that she *had* to leave, not that she *wanted* to, but felt it was the only way to make amends with her parents. She left out the details or the fact that they knew nothing of her plans. She had to try and reach someone – someone she had been told could help her brother. No indication was given as to where she was going, how she would get there, or how long she would be gone. She wasn't sure she wanted things to remain as they were upon her return. She only promised that she would be back and that she cared for him but couldn't stay.

It felt good to make this bold move, and she hoped in time her parents would be proud of her for it. Rachel knew deep down that Jack and Mavis loved her, for they had taken her in and cared for her like their own. They knew nothing of her first three years, and she wondered if they ever would. All she could hope for was that this journey would, in some way, not only help Jon but mend the only family Rachel knew. Maybe some time away would be good for all of them.

Rachel only had about a mile to walk to meet up with an old classmate who had agreed to loan her a horse if she would make a delivery for him. His father raised rare hunting falcons, and a buyer from the Southeastern town of Dahlon had wanted to meet halfway in the centrally located city of Brenton to make the exchange. The young man would have taken the bird himself but they were expecting three hatchlings very soon. His father had told him the importance of being present when they hatched.

They made the arrangements for Rachel to make the delivery and paid her well, even after her protests. She had been setting aside small amounts of money since she had decided to make this journey, but the additional funds were exactly what she needed to secure her plans. The timing was perfect for Rachel too; the ride was a good three days and the delivery was to be made the morning of the fourth day of her trip.

As Rachel made her way down the half-crumbled, cobblestone road, she could just make out her friend arriving in the dim morning light at the arranged meeting place, behind the general store. She greeted Evan with a warm smile, "Thank you for agreeing to loan me the horse."

He was a shy boy with few friends but a heart of gold. He could be trusted to keep the secret of her adventure, but she chose not to tell him everything. It was better if he didn't know the details in case someone questioned him. "Remember, it's best if you stick to the story of the falcon delivery if anyone should ask," Rachel stated.

"I remember. Here…" Evan provided her with a map of the area and showed her where to meet the falcon's buyer.

"Also, I'll be gone longer than just the trip to Brenton and back, but I can't give you an exact return date."

"The gelding is an extra … he won't be missed. Just bring the payment from the falcon upon your return."

The horse that was provided for Rachel was a chestnut that happened to be a comfortable size for her. His eyes met hers. She could sense gentleness there. As she approached, he nuzzled his head to the side of her arm, and she rubbed his cheek. This would be a fine companion. After instructions and arrangements were settled and the bird was secured on a special mount attached to the saddle, Rachel set off due west.

She scanned the area one more time and wiped the nervous sweat from her palms as she mounted up. She wanted to get out of town before anyone realized she was gone. The morning air was brisk and harsh against Rachel's face as she rode; it made her eyes water. She may have pushed the horse too hard too early on. The irritated squawking from the bird clued her in on the fact that they were taking things a bit too fast. She tugged gently on the reins to slow the pace.

The terrain was easy to travel with a wide, gravel road and pines spread out on either side. She tried to stick closer to the old road at the base of the mountains rather than the roads closer to town. After all, it would not do any good for someone to recognize her and delay her mission, or blab to her parents or Lane if they were to come looking for her!

Her eyes closed as emotions bubbled up at the thought of them. Jack and Mavis were already distraught about Jon. What would they do if they found her out?

Never mind that. It's too late to think about that now.

She needed to keep going and only stopped once at midday to venture into a small market where the old and new roads came to a 'Y' at the edge of Brimley Downs for some food. She walked quickly through the vendor booths with excitement tingling through her limbs. The distance from home was encouraging.

After continuing on, Rachel found a secluded area nearly forty miles from her home to settle down for the night. She knew how to ride well enough, but had not often ridden for this long. By the end of her first day of travel, she slowly and gingerly slid from the saddle. Her stiff muscles begged her to stop moving. She brought the falcon down from the saddle and removed the cover from the falcon's cage.

It was a quiet night and felt warmer than it had that morning. There didn't appear to be a cloud in the sky; the stars blinked down at her. She gathered wood for a small fire and set out some fruit and cheese. The scraps of raw meat were unwrapped and carefully fed to the falcon as her friend had instructed.

He was a fierce-looking bird, with wild eyes, and feathers that were so sleek they reflected every flicker of the fire light. She watched him for some time. His eyes shone with intelligence and something else. If she had to come up with a word for him, it would be snobbish. The way the flames danced on his feathers was mesmerizing and soon she realized how tired she was. She unrolled her bed pad and blanket, checked the horse, covered the bird, and lay down. She gazed at the stars, wondering what tomorrow would bring.

TRAVEL DAY TWO

Before opening her eyes, Rachel yawned and stretched. Her hand crashed into something metallic and a shrill squawk startled her. Luckily, she realized what she had hit in time to steady the falcon's cage before the bird could hold too much of a grudge. After he was settled again, and her own heartbeat was back to normal, she got up to douse the last of the embers from last night's fire and get back into the saddle. *Ouch. The saddle.* She wondered if it was too late to turn back, to go back home and hope the local doctors would figure out how to help Jon. No, she couldn't be such a baby, sore or not. Jon needed more than what the local doctors could provide. He needed a healer.

[*Raiza... please...*] A familiar voice pleaded in the back of her mind. She had heard this voice before. It never seemed out of place and always addressed her by the name she called herself as a toddler. It never unnerved her; she figured it was her conscience, but this time it seemed different.

Must be because of my situation. She was alone, except for the falcon and the horse, and she was determined to get help for Jon. She was also feeling a bit scared. This must have been why that little voice sounded so desperate for her to listen. She fiddled with the end of her golden braid for a moment before shrugging off that little voice. She prepared for another day of travel.

With her finger on the map Evan had given her, she planned out her day in her mind. *I only have about thirty miles to travel today. I think we can take things a bit slower. We'll make camp before the bridge that crosses the Rune River into Brenton.*

The feel of the sun warmed Rachel's back as she rode. Even though there was urgency to her trip, she allowed herself to take in and enjoy her surroundings as the horse carried her along.

Occasionally, Lane came to mind. Though they had never gone further than that one kiss, she wondered what could have been if she had stayed. Could she have been happy as his wife? Lane had a moderate-sized goat ranch not far from the Mills'. He would inherit it from his father, as he had from his father before him. They were a well-respected and hardworking family and well established in the community. Once again, she thought to herself, *He's safe*, but was safe really what she wanted?

Deciding to put Lane at the back of her mind and focus on her travels, she began to notice changes to the land. She was breaking away from the base of the Conner Mountains, and as she went, the signs of spring became more evident. Small, colorful birds flitted about in the treetops. Flower buds carefully peeked out of the underbrush. Immature saplings dotted with tiny, light green leaves stretched up between small groups of pine trees. And the air! The air rushed into her lungs as she breathed deeply and marveled at the simple beauty around her.

Muscles rippled on the horse's frame as he plodded along. He was beginning to stray from the gravel road, and she got the hint that it was a good time to take a break. She led the horse to a tiny stream to the left of the road, checked the falcon, and got herself some dried fruit and bread. She watched the horse while he grazed. *I didn't even ask Evan what the horse's name was!* She had had too much on her mind. As she nibbled at the bread, she pondered on what his name could be. She thought of several names and actually made herself chuckle at a few of the more comical ones. The horse gave her a quizzical glance then continued to graze. There wasn't anything particularly special about him – no blaze on his forehead, or socks, or special markings of any kind, just a chestnut.

"That's it," she decided. "I will call you Chestnut." It was a fitting name to match his coloring; she gave his neck a pat.

After a good rest and something to eat, they were back on the road. Chestnut must have been well rested because he began to trot. Her backside felt no comfort in the action, but the slight breeze lifted small tendrils of hair and cooled Rachel's face and neck. They continued on, switching between a trot and a walk. There were few others on this route. Most stayed to themselves with the occasional nod toward Rachel.

As early evening approached, Rachel could see a great deal of movement and some small campfires just off the road about two hundred yards ahead. She slowed Chestnut and began to feel uneasy. No one so far had given her any trouble, but this was a big group and she didn't want to assume all fellow travelers were friendly. Guessing there were twenty-five or more people ahead, she made sure her dagger was handy and her cargo was secure.

Music? Was she hearing music, and laughter? Yes, it was coming from the group ahead. The end of her braid was between her fingers as she looped it back and forth. Taking a deep breath, she let the strands drop from her fingers. Sudden nerves made it difficult to swallow as she began to approach the others.

The group was not quite as large as Rachel had originally thought. They were all just moving about, dancing, singing, juggling, and tumbling. As Rachel approached, it was as if the whole show had been planned for her. The performers didn't miss a beat, just continued around her. Whirling and spinning bodies and laughter surrounded her. If they hadn't been so merry, she may have felt overwhelmed. Instead, she felt like joining in! Chestnut wasn't even bothered by them. The falcon, on the other hand, probably would have rolled his eyes in disdain if he could have. Rachel dismounted and the introductions began.

First, a very large and burley man with thick, wavy, salt and pepper hair stepped forward. Rachel, with her petite frame, and only five feet four inches tall, felt small in his presence. He towered over her by more than a foot and had broad shoulders, bulging biceps, and a beaming smile.

"The name's Bram, I'm the leader of the group." Next to be introduced was Bram's wife,

Sierra, a tall beautiful woman in her middle-aged years, with flowing, golden brown hair past her waist. She stood next to Bram and came just below his chin. The way he looked at her, like she was the only woman to exist, melted Rachel's heart. One by one, the rest of the eighteen members of the group introduced themselves. There were nine men and nine women in total: actors, dancers, tumblers, musicians, and crew.

They offered Rachel to join them for the evening. When she tried to decline the offer, they wouldn't take no for an answer. Truth be told, she really didn't want to leave them anyway.

Everyone chipped in to raise two large tents and start a good-sized cooking fire. Old logs were brought around for seating. While they waited for drinks to be passed around and meats to be roasted, the conversations began.

Bram inquired about Rachel's journey. "Where are you heading? And why are you traveling alone?" There was concern in his voice even though they had just met. He reminded her of her father in that way.

Not wanting to tell too much of her reasons for her journey, she told him she was continuing west just a short way after delivering the falcon in

Brenton. "I assure you, it should c
days." Bram considered her for
leaned back with a nod. It wasn't ;
just left out a few things. She quickly ..
questions, "What about you guys? Where are yo..
headed?"

They explained that they had come from
Brenton and were heading to Brimley.

"There is to be a great feast for King
Stephan," Sierra began.

"Put on *by* King Stephan," interrupted one of
the performers.

"In the palace..." Sierra continued with a
playful glare in the direction of the interruption. "We
have been there many times before and the job pays
well."

They were not shy about admitting their
disdain for the king as they continued. "Stephan has
ruled for nearly twenty years, with his mommy at his
side – no wife, no queen, no children."

"At least none that were legitimate," scoffed
one of the dancers.

That statement was immediately followed by,
"That's just not right," from one of the musicians,

laughter and murmured agreement from the
others. It was difficult for Rachel to keep up with the
others as their comments overlapped one another.

Life in Brimley had been prosperous for most
when the predecessor, King Desmond, had ruled,
even in his later years when he ruled in sorrow. At
least his people didn't suffer. Stephan was
Desmond's cousin and took over the throne after
Desmond had died. The kingdom had not been the
same since. More often than not, Stephan turned to
his mother, Lady Jillian, for advice. She was a
greedy woman and would advise Stephan to raise
taxes and tolls throughout the land. Taxation,
although necessary, when the proceeds find their
way into the pockets of the corrupt, is abhorred.

When King Desmond held the throne, the
taxes for each region were kept within the
community whence they came, with only a small
percentage of the proceeds sent to the castle. There
were taxes placed upon property owners that were
used for common needs such as road upkeep,
education costs, and medical expenses. Those in the
community who could not afford to own their own
property had a smaller portion of their income set
aside for tax. The system was fair, and there were
few complaints.

Soon after Stephen had taken the crown from his cousin, things began to change. No longer were the funds collected and used in each town. He claimed there had been misuse of those funds and demanded they be sent directly to the castle to be dispersed as he saw fit. The settlements were now receiving back only a portion of their collected monies, the rest being squandered on those closest to the king.

Farmers and ranchers were not only taxed on their lands but on their goods: crops, livestock, pelts, and wool. Fishermen too were taxed on their boats and their catch. Sometimes, depending on the season, these taxations made it difficult to profit enough to support their families. In addition to this, the roads were not well kept, making travel difficult. If these merchants could not travel easily, they could not conduct business as needed, selling and trading services with other nearby merchants.

The amenities, once taken for granted, were now sorely missed. Schools and medical facilities with qualified instructors and doctors were once a common sight in each town, but no longer. Because of funds being held back, the schools were being closed and the doctors relocated to more populated areas that could continue to provide for their services.

There was an underlying depression to the population of Eagle Island. If people couldn't pay their taxes with coin, they were made to pay in other ways. They were forced to leave their homes and spend terms in work camps near the palace, or sent to wither in the castle prison. Rachel hadn't seen it first hand, due to her young age, but had heard how good life was before. She tried to imagine how it had affected the Mills or even Lane's family. But what could be done about it?

Not wanting the sour mood to continue, Sierra began to tell Rachel of the more enjoyable parts of their past visits to the palace. She went into great detail about the Grand Hall where they performed.

"The room is roughly one hundred feet in width and almost three times that in length. The arched ceiling high above is trimmed with ornately carved stone tiles depicting symbols of the four elements: fire, water, earth, and wind. The tiles of fire have gold leafing on the raised edges of the flames; the gold catches the sunlight by day and sparkles in the myriad of candles by night. The water tiles have been glazed to appear always wet and quite possibly have been inlaid with sapphire dust in the carving's depths. They simply sparkle. Vines, branches, leaves, and stones decorate the earthen tiles. Lastly, my favorite, the air tiles have abstract swirling patterns in shades of silver and lavender and are so delicate they appear transparent. The artist who created them must have been quite special. I could stare at the ceiling of the Grand Hall for the rest of my days and count myself content.

"There is an enormous fireplace at the south end with slabs of stone veined with crystals. I promise you, it could hold at least two bull elk for roasting, and still have room for kettles of vegetable stew! The balcony, for the minstrels, has a northerly facing window behind it to let in natural daylight. It looks out over the clifftops to the sea… breathtaking. The colorful, stained-glass windows that are set high above seem to come to life when the sun shines through them, casting an array of colors down to dance upon the polished, marble floor tiles."

She continued on to describe the extravagant tapestries that adorned the walls. "Even though they depict scenes of Lady Jillian surrounded by servants or 'adoring' common folk or King Stephan in battle or on his steed, they are beautifully done with rich colors and fine detailing.

"In past trips, servants would prepare our rooms with fresh flowers along with bowls of ripe fruit, and sugared fruit candies. It truly is an amazing experience."

Rachel could almost see the hall in her mind and smell the fresh flowers. Though she had never had sugared fruit candies before, she could imagine the delight of eating them. Her mouth watered.

Eric, one of the musicians that appeared just a little older than Rachel, joined the conversation. He was tall and lean, and his jet-black hair was tied neatly at the nape of his neck. He began telling her about the fountain that was inside the Great Hall, just before the doors on the west side of the gardens.

She listened to the lilt of his smooth voice. The way he described everything was like a song leading her imagination through the garden doors. The words carried her over the stone pathway with golden, orange, and red tones that resembled the setting sun, and into the lush greenery of the gardens themselves. The low hedge maze he described was obviously made for meandering through and not to get one lost. Everything they described to her sounded wonderful.

She couldn't help longing to go there. Although Rachel's home was only a two-day ride from the palace, she had never been there. Most people hadn't since Stephan became king. He was not as welcoming as his cousin had been.

Rachel inwardly cursed King Desmond's situation. *If he hadn't done whatever it was that landed him in the dungeons, I might have been able to see the palace someday.* Even though King Stephan had taken the throne in her lifetime, history had not held Rachel's attention in school.

As the evening went on and everyone had their meal eaten and their beds prepared, one by one the performers went to their tents to sleep. Bram, Sierra, Eric and the twin acrobats, Charlie and Chorale, stayed up for a bit longer sharing more stories with Rachel.

Charlie was on the ground stretching and telling Rachel about the main play the cast would perform for the king and his guests. Chorale would interrupt now and then to add details or something he had left out. It was amusing to Rachel that Charlie never got flustered by her interruptions, just kept going as if they had done this a million times. She wasn't sure why she was so intrigued by it, but it made her smile. She felt Eric slide a little closer on the log they shared, and he offered her part of his blanket for her shoulders. She took it with a smile and continued to watch and listen to the twin acrobats who, by this time, had become quite animated in their storytelling.

Bram and Sierra smiled at each other, then at Charlie and Chorale. Giving a little wave, they excused themselves to their tent. Not long afterwards, Chorale nudged Charlie and suggested they do the same. They had finished their story and had seen something Rachel had missed. Eric had been giving silent cues to the others that he wanted to spend a little more time with Rachel and not the rest of them.

Suddenly, Rachel and Eric were alone in the dim light of the fire. Rachel felt uneasy. Eric made a bold move to reach over and take hold of Rachel's hand. "I would very much like it if we could meet up again when you return," (from what he thought was a 'short journey'). "You seem to have captured my heart. I'm drawn to you in a way I can't quite explain."

Rachel was taken aback by his advances but also a bit flattered. He was handsome enough, and well spoken. She thought that if things had been different, she might have taken him up on that offer. But Rachel knew she would not be returning home in a few days and their paths may never cross again. "I don't know what to say ..." She paused in thought.

Eric leaned in toward her.

She backed away and looked down at her hand in his. "I'm terribly flattered but I don't know that I will be home before you and the others are done at the palace."

He looked at her first with confusion then understanding as she told him there was more to her journey that she wasn't comfortable sharing. He backed away for a moment then leaned in again, almost uncomfortably close, and whispered, "You're heading farther west than you mentioned, aren't you? How far west?"

"How did you know?" Rachel asked with a hint of panic in her words.

"When Bram asked about your journey, you mentioned it, but then stopped. I couldn't help but notice," Eric began. "The sailors on the western piers have a bad reputation; I hope you don't plan on going that way on your own. It isn't safe. No offense meant, but you don't exactly have the appearance of someone who can take on the world. Do you even have a weapon to defend yourself?" Eric's concern was evident in his eyes.

Rachel truly didn't know what she would be up against, but she had to take the risk. "I understand your concern, but really, I will be fine," she tried to sound convincing despite her own uncertainty.

"I could go with you to keep you safe!" he blurted. "I'm sure the group wouldn't miss me too badly, and I can catch up to them upon our return. Please, Rachel ... allow me this." He didn't want her to go alone. Truthfully, he didn't want her to leave, period.

As he spoke, he remained close, so close Rachel wondered if he would try to kiss her. She did not want to involve anyone else, to put anyone else in danger, or to find herself in another one-sided relationship. What was it about these men? She certainly didn't consider herself one for men to throw themselves at. She was small, blond with blue eyes, not ugly – she supposed – but lacked the grace and confidence she had seen in others girls, and never considered herself any great beauty. She was a simple girl.

Quickly she thought of a lie, hopefully one to let him down gently and get out of this awkward closeness. "I'm going to the piers of Brenton to find my ex-boyfriend. He left me suddenly ... to find work at the docks and I need closure. It wouldn't be appropriate for me to bring another man. I don't have far to go. I will be careful. I'm sorry, Eric."

With that, Rachel removed her hand from his and bid him a good night. She felt guilty and could no longer look him in the eye. Once again, the end of her braid found its way to her fingers as she headed for her bedroll.

Eric watched her walk away. His brows were pinched. His stare could have bored a hole through her. Obviously, she had more on her mind and wanted to deal with it on her own, so he held in any protest he had.

Merri Gammage

TRAVEL DAY THREE

Breakfast the next morning was quiet, and the air was chilly again; spring was never predictable. The traveling entertainers packed everything up and said their goodbyes to Rachel, leaving Eric for last.

"Are you sure I can't change your mind? I could OK it with Bram right now before we head out. I could escort you safely to your destination then remain out of sight when you find your ex-boyfriend. He will never need to know I was there," Eric attempted to convince her one last time.

"Eric," she began with a sigh. "I have already made up my mind, and I'm sorry, this is something I must do on my own. Thank you again, for your concern, but no."

The crestfallen look on Eric's face was enough to make Rachel's stomach sour, but the look changed to that of resignation as he nodded and leaned in for a hug. She did not shy away from his embrace but was the first to step away from its warmth. She turned to leave. He just stood there, staring at her. She and Chestnut galloped away until she was far enough that she felt no one would follow. Glancing back, to make sure she was indeed alone, she slowed the horse to a walk.

Today, she would cross the great bridge over the Rune River. The bridge was wide and sturdy and had been built when former King Desmond was a young prince. The towns of Brimley, Brenton, Dahlon, and Traither had commissioned their strongest men to construct the bridge for all to use. The originally small toll collected would be divided fairly amongst the towns for road repairs or town betterments. But now the fairly large toll was collected and sent right to King Stephan. The bridge was just a few more miles ahead.

When they got there, Rachel dismounted Chestnut and got out her coins. The guards that were posted on either side of the bridge would inquire about the reason for crossing; the falcon gave her a valid reason to cross. The coins clinked together as the bag jostled from one hand to the other while she waited to pay. She bit her cheek nervously. Would they ask more questions about the duration of her stay, or why she had more than enough packed for such a short journey? *If they ask, I'll tell them it is my first trip like this. I would rather have it and not need it, than need it and not have it! It is the truth anyway, sort of.*

As she gave the guard her coins, his far-away gaze showed he could not have cared one bit about her stay, her travels, how much she packed; he just wanted to collect the coins and get her moving. When she paused to ask him about possible lodging inside Brenton, the guard raised his eyes to the sky, rolled them, sighed and grunted, "Ask on the other side, lady!" as if he had already been questioned one too many times that morning.

"All right, all right, sorry," she retorted and stepped ahead, leading Chestnut.

Crossing took Rachel nearly half an hour, not because the river was exceptionally wide, but because of the number of people filtering through in both directions. She had never seen anything like it. There were merchants of every sort on the bridge, traveling between the towns. They had colorful fabrics, baskets of fish, wheels and wedges of cheeses, livestock, and other items to sell or trade.

She was, at times, just standing in awe until someone would protest. It may have only taken ten minutes to cross if it had been just her and Chestnut.

Rachel didn't want to bother the guards on this side too since there seemed to be more people waiting to cross into Brimley than the other way around. After stepping off the bridge, she decided to ask a woman about accommodations in Brenton. The woman seemed to be alone and was strolling at a leisurely pace. "Excuse me, ma'am? Can you point me toward a place to stay for the evening?"

"Head that way," she pointed with a huff.

Not a very friendly type, Rachel thought.

"I'm new in town. What about travel supplies, food and such? One more thing … I'm to meet someone at 'Eagle's Head Inn' tomorrow. Is that also in this direction?" Rachel asked next, indicating the same direction the lady had pointed.

She kept her answers short, "Head for the V. They got everything: food, supplies, lodging, and yes, the inn too."

"Thank you," Rachel called to the back of the lady's head as she continued on her way.

Eagle Island was positioned in the Ezra Sea to the East of Paradiso, on the mainland. It got its name from its shape, loosely resembling an eagle in flight. Situated on the *head* and *neck* of said eagle (or the northwest quadrant of the island) was the fishing town of Brenton. Compared to Brimley Heights, located on the *shoulder* of the right *wing* (or northern-most part of the island), Brenton was the second largest of the island communities.

Brenton had an interesting layout. The north part of town, the *beak* and *head*, jutted out into the sea with piers on either side. A bit inland were the main shops and lodging, arranged in a V with the point toward the sea. It was in the row of shops that made up the northern leg of the V that Rachel found the inn just before noon. She decided to go in and check the rates. It was way out of her price range. She already knew this by looking at the place; it was beautifully decorated. Further inland, on the *neck*, were the smaller shops and homes. She decided to head that direction to a row of small cottages just down a side road from the Eagle's Head. Rachel noticed the style of the cottages seemed very much like the inn and hoped they weren't the employees' living quarters or something similar. She had no clue how those things worked. As she got a little closer, there was a plump woman sweeping the sandy path just in front of the first cottage.

She looked up at Rachel with a smile and slapped the dust off her hands as she approached her. "Good morning, I'm Lynette, proprietor of the Golden Eagle Cottages," the lady introduced herself. "Are you in need of lodging? I've got one available cottage two doors down, with a single-stalled stable for a horse."

"That sounds perfect – if the price is right," Rachel smiled.

After hearing the low rate, she paid Lynette and got the tour. The cottage was fairly small but modern. Upon entering, the kitchen area and cooking fire were to the right. Directly ahead was a pocket door that led to the bathing room, and directly to the left was another pocket door that led to the bedroom. The fireplace was made out of large, rounded stones and had been kept very tidy, with wood stacked in the corner next to it.

Lynette was very particular about the fireplace, "The ash needs to be emptied when you leave," a stern gaze fixed Rachel in her spot for a moment before they continued.

The bathing room was nicer than most Rachel had been in with a tub and sink that had a pump for water from a nearby hot spring and a toilet (certainly better than squatting outside). Up above, near the ceiling, was a small window for daylight and torches mounted along the walls for evening lighting. Lynette then motioned her hand toward the bedroom and Rachel noticed a hint of pride on her face. She quickly understood when she saw the quilt on the bed. The colors were more vivid than Rachel was used to and sewn in a simple pattern that showcased each panel.

Rachel stepped in and ran her hands along the quilt, examining its pattern. "You made this?" she asked. "It's the finest I've ever seen!" she added when Lynette answered with a nod.

Lynette blushed slightly as she waved her hands about. "Oh, come now! I just want my guests to be warm and feel welcomed." Lynette then explained to Rachel that she ran the cottages and her sister ran the inn. "We own them together and strategically built the cottages for the *more average budget.*" She and Rachel conversed for a bit longer and Rachel found her to be quite a personable woman. Lynette excused herself to finish her duties and let Rachel settle in.

After Rachel had secured the falcon in her room and unpacked some of her belongings, she made arrangements for Chestnut to be groomed, at a minimal added cost. It was time to head into town for a late lunch and some supplies.

Brenton was quite busy. In addition to the normal shops, there was a farmers' market being held in the grassy area that was the center of the V. Rachel thought about the small market in her hometown, remembering the many days she had spent with her family selling wool and vegetables. She enjoyed perusing the different items for sale, some of which she had never seen before. She knew Brimley Heights had much larger shops and such, but her family lead a simple life outside the heart of the city.

When she came around the south leg of the V, her eyes closed and her mouth watered; she could smell fresh fish being smoked nearby. She decided to follow that scent in hopes there would be some to purchase. The smokehouse was less than halfway down, and they not only had fresh and smoked fish but other meats, such as mutton and goose, and some leather goods. She was tempted to spend more than she did, but Rachel had rationed out enough coins to pay for a sampling to add to her supplies and a leather satchel large enough to hold her food items. As it was now, she had all her belongings in one bag; she was quite pleased to have something to keep her food separate from her bedroll.

Rachel continued back the way she came, realizing the far end of that half of the V seemed to be reserved for ale houses. Those she would seek out later in hopes of getting further information for her journey. She continued to shop. It was a beautiful afternoon, and Rachel had not been to the seashore that she could remember. She decided to sit at a table at the apex of the V where there was covered seating. Others were doing the same with friends or family to take a break. She ate a small loaf, some of the smoked fish, and a wedge of cheese she had purchased as she gazed about.

The salty air gently fluttered her golden hair as small wisps escaped her braid. Gulls dipped and drifted above the sand and piers hoping for a scrap from the fishermen's nets as they cleaned them before heading back out. To her left, a young mother cooed at her little one and to her right, a man and what appeared to be his son practiced knot tying. Ahead of her she could hear the murmurs of the fishermen as they called out orders or playfully harassed their neighbor about how much more of a catch each one had. She sat dazed, taking it all in.

THUNK!

Rachel woke with a start; she had drifted off and after about an hour, her head had lulled forward to collide with the tabletop. This was not her favorite way to wake up. Looking around, then down at her new belongings, she was relieved about two things: one, that no one had seemed to notice her and two, all of her items were exactly as she had left them when she sat down. Judging by the muted colors in the sky, it would be sunset soon. It was time to head back to the cottage. Chestnut and the falcon would be ready for their evening meal.

When she arrived at the cottage, Rachel lit a fire and fed her companions, taking a moment to tell the falcon she wished him well and that she would miss him. He wasn't as kind or personable as Chestnut, but she thought he was a beautiful and regal creature. She carefully rubbed the back of her index finger on the feathers near his neck, unsure of how he would respond. After a moment, he leaned into the affectionate gesture. Once he had had enough, he shifted to the side away from her, so she closed the cage and covered it for the night. She was exhausted, but transferred her food items into her new satchel before lying down for the night.

Once the business with the falcon was completed in the morning, she'd have time to gather information. Her mind raced with anticipation.

TRAVEL DAY FOUR

The next morning came sooner than Rachel wanted. She woke with a gentle sadness tugging at her heart. She had dreamt of her family, the only family she had known, and wondered if they were worried about her. Would they be searching for her? She knew it had only been a few days, but it felt like more; she missed them. The quilt was warm and soft on her cheek as she tugged it closer to her body for comfort. Since she and the Mills had not been in daily contact, she doubted they would be looking for her yet. That helped to ease the sadness.

She got up and started a fire to heat some oatmeal, fed the falcon with some scraps of fresh mutton she had acquired from the market, and took a step outside to check on Chestnut. When she placed her head on his neck, he nudged her and pressed his forehead to her cheek. It was as if he could sense her mood. This trip had been more physically and emotionally taxing on her than she anticipated. She reluctantly went back inside to eat and then took the falcon to the inn to meet up with his new owner.

Rachel arrived first and couldn't remember the man's name. Evan had told her she wouldn't be able to mistake him; he was shorter than her and almost as wide as he was tall. Soon, she saw a man she was sure to be the one. As he waddled up to her, she had to bite her lip to avoid a giggle at his expense. He was a very round man with red cheeks, small bright eyes, and dimples. His curly, strawberry hair bounced as he walked and he huffed a bit with each step. He was dressed in fine clothing, even if it didn't quite fit him properly. She could tell he was a kind man, and he seemed thrilled with the bird. Rachel was not able to stifle the giggle when the man began speaking to the bird in a comical manner as if trying to make a toddler smile. The bird ruffled his neck feathers at the sound.

When the corners of the man's mouth turned down into a sad frown, Rachel placed a reassuring hand on his forearm. "He seems to like to be stroked here, on his neck ... like this." She showed him, and the falcon responded pleasantly. When the man tried it, the bird leaned in, bringing a smile to his pudgy face. The sale was finalized with no haggling, to Rachel's relief; she wasn't prepared for that. They bid each other farewell and Rachel went back to the cottage to hide the considerably-sized coin purse from the sale before she set out back to town.

Without raising too much suspicion, Rachel needed some details about how to get to Geerda. She knew the basic area she needed to get to, but after that, it was a bit of a mystery. The map Evan had provided did not stretch that far west. She secured her dagger and hid some extra money to barter with if needed. As she got herself ready, Rachel's thoughts bounced between her destination and her brother.

Having contact with the elven village had been forbidden for over one hundred years. Talking about it hadn't been restricted (at least not yet) as long as it was kept quiet. Rachel had heard several hushed conversations about the village when she was in school. She knew that elves were banned from traveling into the two main northern human towns of Brenton and Brimley. They were not encouraged in the smaller southern towns of Dahlon and Traither either, but people there had more of a tolerance toward them. In addition to that, humans were forbidden from seeking out the aid of the elves for magical or healing purposes. Rachel was not sure what had started the separation but was always told it was best to just stay away from the elves and their magic. That, of course, made her more curious ... and anxious, especially now.

When the doctors in Brimley had told the Mills there was little else that could be done for Jon, they were devastated. They tried herbal remedies and every medicine the doctors could think of. Some would work to aid with pain relief, only to cause sleeplessness, or some would help him sleep but cause his fever to spike. No one could determine the cause of his illness or how to cure it. They weren't sure how long he had left to live. Seeing Jon so miserable nearly broke Rachel's heart. He seemed most comfortable when Rachel held him, but she felt helpless.

Thoughts buzzed through Rachel's mind. The specific conversation that sparked the idea for this journey came to the forefront. She had decided to go along with Lane to the farmers market to sell some goat cheese. She ran into one of the girls from school who had been discussing Geerda. She was a quiet girl, but friendly and always willing to help people.

"Dawn! It's been a while. How are you?" Rachel asked as the former classmate stood patiently beside her mother who was shopping the market.

"Hello Rachel. I'm good, thank you." She placed a warm hand on Rachel's. "How have you been? I heard your brother is ill … I hope it's not too serious?" she inquired quietly.

"Oh Dawn, it's bad. The doctors are baffled," Rachel fought back her emotions. "We aren't sure where else to turn. Nothing seems to help."

"Lane, we'll be right back … Rachel, come over here for a moment," she quickly pulled Rachel aside for some privacy. Dawn kept her voice low. "Have you thought about asking the elves in Geerda? They have healers. I know we're not supposed to … but if you go to them, I'm told they are usually willing to help. Don't be fooled by those old stories of them being devils and such. My aunt has occasional dealings with them and says they really aren't any different from us, except for their abilities. I think it would be worth a try," Dawn whispered with an urgency Rachel could hardly ignore. Dawn's mother waved to her that she was done, and moved on to the next booth. "Let me know if you need more information. At least think about it," she said as she left.

Rachel had pondered the idea of going to Geerda for nearly a month before deciding to embark upon this journey. Dawn provided what little information she could, but it wasn't enough. Her aunt was not willing to divulge her contact information to her niece. It was just too dangerous. Now Rachel needed details to get her to the path that led through the ancient forest between Mt. Spire and Geerda; the thought made her shudder. There were many rumors of ghosts, dark magic and strange creatures that lurked in that forest. She was sure it would be the most daunting part of her journey.

Rachel left her cottage and headed south just a couple streets over. She had asked Lynette if there was an herbalist nearby. Herbalists usually dabbled in at least a little bit of magic, even if they didn't openly admit it, and maybe she could draw some clues out of one of them. When she found the shop, she opened the door and stepped inside. An elderly man sat on a stool at the front counter of the small building. Except for the bundles of herbs covering the wall, it was similar to the cottage she stayed in. To the right, a cauldron bubbled away on the fire, with the steam smelling of mint and other soothing herbs. There looked to be a pocket door directly behind the man and another to the left. She wondered if he was living there as well as selling his herbal remedies.

He welcomed her in and asked what she was after. Knowing there would be trouble if she came right out and told him she was trying to get to Geerda or the elves, she instead told him a half-truth;

it tugged at her soul to think she was becoming deft at telling them. She asked him for a fever reducer for her little brother. It was a common item so he had small pre-bundled batches and produced one from under the counter in no time. She had to think of something to get a conversation going so she asked about what was in the cauldron.

He smiled and nodded to acknowledge it. "It's a secret recipe of herbs to refresh the air and calm the mind."

"It certainly seems to work," she confessed.

She was having a hard time coming up with more questions that might lead to small talk or more information. She stood there and fiddled nervously with her coins. The man looked at her, with brows up, waiting for payment or closure to their transaction. She shrugged and handed him the coins. Silently, she cursed herself for not having a better plan as she stepped toward the door.

[*Raiza ... can you hear me?*] She heard the little voice ask.

Of course I can 'hear you', she thought to herself, a bit puzzled as to why her own conscience would ask such a question. Then, by some miracle, she remembered an herb she had seen in the market by her home for a sleep aid but also its flowers were used for perfume. The lady at the market had told her it grew close to the old forest by the sea. She whirled around, "Do you have any valerian root or know where I could get some?"

Again, the man smiled, pulled a bundle from under the counter. "No charge," he offered, figuring it was for her brother.

"Please, take this," she held out a coin but he shook his head in refusal.

"No, no … it's easy to find and not worth the extra coin." That was the 'in' she needed for more information.

"Do you think the flowers are good for perfume? Could you tell me where it grows?"

He thought for a moment, rubbing his chin. "A woman I knew had used it for perfume once, but it was not a scent I cared for, so I had not given it much consideration after that …" As his voice trailed off, she wondered if that was the end of it, but then he perked up again and continued. "There are several wild plants by the far west end of town before the entrance of the …" With this, his voice lowered and he leaned in, as if someone else were listening, and finished by whispering, "the entrance to the forest, just south of the piers ... but you best not go alone and only during the daylight you know." Then he resumed his prior tone and posture and asked, "Is there anything else you needed?"

"No, thank you. I think that will be all," and she excused herself.

That was a lucky thing to remember! Now she had her direct route to the forest. There was still almost a full day ahead of her, so she decided to find out more about the secretive forest she intended to travel through. Maybe she would get lucky again and get even more information, maybe even something about the elves.

She headed back to the main part of town to check out the ale house patrons. This early in the day, it would most likely be regulars and older folks. Since it was the end of the work week, there might be a bit rougher crowd later in the evening. She wanted to avoid that crowd. The first place she entered seemed fairly nice and bright inside, but not a soul sat at the bar or the few scattered tables.

A young man stepped out from the back, behind the bar. "We don't officially open ..." he started as he looked her over, "for another few hours, peach, but can I help you?"

She didn't get the feeling he really meant it in a way to welcome a customer. By the way he puffed up his chest and eyeballed her from top to bottom, it looked more like he wanted something from her.

"No, thank you. Sorry!" she called over her shoulder as she made a hasty exit. She heard him chuckle, shook off his offensive gaze and kept going.

The next bar, a few doors down, offered a bit more promise. She went inside to find several patrons catching up with each other or reliving old times, old fishermen and women she guessed. They were rough around the edges but seemed kind enough. Most of the men had scraggly facial hair and tattoos. The women were mostly thin with lean muscles. All of them had tanned, leathery skin.

Rachel sat at a table within earshot of a large group of people who certainly seemed as if they had *been around.* When the bar maid approached, Rachel asked for a beer, some broth, and bread as she began to eavesdrop on the group next to her. It wasn't a difficult task. They were not, by any means, soft-spoken. Their words overlapped one another's and were peppered with curses.

They spoke of old times when life was easier and their catch brought more coin. One man began to grumble about how it was the "mother-loving-king's" fault for it all, and the others agreed. Rachel, wondering how long it would take for her order to arrive, heard her own voice echoing the others in the conversation before she could stop herself. "Isn't that the truth …" she muttered louder than she had meant to. She had heard her own family hint at the situation and remembered the entertainers had had the same dislike for their king. She hoped her intrusion wouldn't cause trouble with the group. As they slowly turned to gaze in her direction with unreadable expressions, she felt her hands begin to sweat from nerves.

"I'm sorry. I didn't mean to eavesdrop. It's just that … well … it's no secret now, is it?" she apologized and put her hands up, smiling shyly.

The man sitting nearest to her gave her a stern look then suddenly clapped her on the shoulder and belted out a laugh. Soon the rest of the table roared with laughter and Rachel exhaled in relief. "It is good to know it isn't just us old dogs that aren't happy with that dismal excuse for a king. Holt," and he offered his hand.

Rachel introduced herself as her broth and bread arrived and the group turned their chairs out some to include her at their table. Before she knew it, talk drifted to the old forest. How could she be this lucky? She didn't even have to ask about it! Several vague stories were shared and each one brought about another, but so far nothing that would specifically help Rachel. The stories were interesting though, full of rumors and gossip.

Now on her second beer, Rachel tried not to look suddenly more interested in the woman who was currently sharing. Had her name been given upon Rachel's introduction to the group? She couldn't remember. The woman was thin, probably in her sixties, with a long, grey braid past her waist. Her skin looked like soft, tanned leather. Her voice sounded like a scrub with fine grit sandpaper. It made Rachel want to clear her throat.

She told of a time when she was young and her mother brought her to the piers to meet with her father.

"He should have been back from a fishing trip off the west coast of Geerda, by the cliffs, but his crew had been delayed. There were several of us there … women and children, waiting in the dark. Upon his return, he told my mother they had been sailing back to the docks when they noticed 'folks that are not spoken of' on the cliffs. The elves," she whispered in explanation, with her hand by her mouth like it made a difference somehow, and then continued. "He told of how they must have been practicing some bad magic or something and there was fire and colored flashes in the sky. The commotion distracted the captain enough to cause him to steer the boat too close to the cliffs. It struck on the rocks below the water's surface. The men were thrown overboard as the boat sank, most of them not making it to the rocky shore. My pop would have to find a new boat to work on, come morning. The few men who did survive had to head east through the forest to get back. While they traveled, they were haunted by spirits, had eyes constantly peering at them through the dark, and noises no one could explain threatened them from behind. These men were no cowards, but that forest had dark magic grown in the roots of those trees; no one ventured in there voluntarily," the woman told her small audience. The barmaid brought out another round.

The old woman finished her story. "After we had heard his tale, we made our way home. But I can still remember some of them other wives and children. They waited there with hope in their eyes, past the last pier, where the old road from the forest came out to meet up with the newer roads of Brenton, waited to collect their men, those that survived, and bring them home safely. I could hear the wailing of a couple of them ... no doubt being told their husbands hadn't made it ... made me squeeze my pop's hand even tighter." There was an odd silence when she finished.

Bingo! Rachel had what she needed, along with the chills. *Past the last pier, where the old road from the forest came out to meet up with the newer roads of Brenton. That's where I'm headed.*

The door of the bar opened and Rachel could see outside. It was later than she had suspected. The sun had set. With a shake to clear her buzzing head, she thanked the old fishermen and women for their company and left the bar. There was a definite chill in the air.

As Rachel passed the first bar she had looked into earlier, her stomach dropped. The bartender who had eyeballed her was exiting with another man. He stopped his loud bawling of a not-so-nice song when he noticed her.

His elbow jabbed his buddy in the side as he slurred, "There's the pretty peach. Let's see how juicy she is!"

Rachel's face contorted in disgust and she glanced at the other, larger man, to gauge his response. He was obviously less drunk, but she doubted he would be any less crude. The bartender was a mid-sized man, possibly a few years her senior, with nothing notable about his features. He had dull brown, unkempt hair and hadn't shaved recently. His companion was disgusting to look upon. Rachel didn't take the time to guess how old he was. She doubted he had ever cleaned his half rotten teeth. His clothing was stained and ill fitting. His hair was greasy and cut poorly.

He raised one eyebrow, belched, and half his mouth curved into a sly smile as he replied, "The juicier the better!"

Oh, great. Two perverts! "You won't be getting close enough to find out!" she spat at them, hoping to look tough enough to hold her own.

In reality, her whole insides were shaking. Unpleasant thoughts of what they might try raced through her mind. She had never had to deal with people like this and was already sure she never wanted to again.

The men took a couple steps closer, and Rachel decided to produce her dagger. She had only used it for amusement in the past, skewering rats back home, but she was fairly handy with it. She convinced herself these men were merely larger rats. If nothing else, she could put out one of their eyes and try to run.

The bartender feigned fear as he continued closer. "Please, dearie, don't put up a fight, with your menacing tiny dagger ..." Then, glancing back at his friend, added with a laugh, "We can pick our teeth with that after we finish the peach."

"Get back!" Rachel yelled, hoping someone might hear and come to a lady's aid. This part of town didn't seem to be where the gentlemen or hero-types frequented though.

Rachel was surprised when the slob grabbed the bartender's arm and pulled him back a pace or two. She did not yet relax. Her heart was racing. The bartender punched at his friend but missed and complained that he 'wanted that peach', but the second man was pointing to their right. When Rachel followed his finger, there was another man approaching. It was too dark to see the look on his face or to know his intentions. Rachel panicked. The original drunk had a goofy grin on his face. Would she now have to fight off three of them?

The approaching man bellowed out one word. "GET!"

The other two must have known who he was and that he meant it. The look of panic ghosted over their faces, their eyes staring fearfully into the darkness. They left in a hurry, tripping over each other as they went. When Rachel looked back toward the approaching man, he was in the torchlight. She recognized him as one of her new friends from the bar she had spent the day at. Holt was much taller than he had appeared while sitting at the table. His large stature commanded respect.

"You unharmed?" he asked. "This is no place to linger after dark. You'd best head to wherever you are staying," he added kindly.

"I'm not hurt. They didn't get the chance, thanks to you... I'll be on my way. Thank you!" She hurried to her cottage, glancing over her shoulder as she tried to calm her nerves. By now, she had completely sobered up. Her stomach clenched.

When she got back to the cottage, she quickly checked on Chestnut and went inside. She picked out the clothing she would wear the following day, packed up everything else she wouldn't need the next morning, and got into bed. She lay awake, twisting the ends of her hair for some time. She couldn't stop thinking of everything she had learned, and what she had just been through. The quilt Lynette had made acted like a warm hug she desperately needed.

Merri Gammage

TRAVEL DAY FIVE

Rachel woke early, bathed, had some breakfast, fed Chestnut, and cleaned the ash from the fireplace as Lynette had requested. She loaded her gear onto Chestnut, bid Lynette a quick thank you and farewell, then traveled back the same way she had come home from the bar the night before. She felt uneasy and prayed to avoid any trouble. Daylight should deter some of the less honorable citizens from the previous night. She had to focus on her journey now. She knew where to go based on the information from the herbalist and the lady at the bar. Chestnut surely must have felt her tension. He kept swinging his head back to try to brush her knee and get her attention. When she finally realized what he was doing, she let herself relax a bit and patted his neck to reassure him she would be OK.

"Let's just get through today and find that road," she said aloud.

Luckily, they had no troubles making their way through Brenton. As she rode west, there were rows of homes to her left with the market place to her right. The people who were out and about were pleasant, if not friendly, nodding casual greetings to one another as they went about their day. Rachel and Chestnut stopped briefly for a rest and a bit to eat. Chestnut nibbled at the tender spring grasses near the roadside as Rachel picked through her rations. The going was the same once she was mounted back into the saddle and continued west. They made it to the last pier before dark.

Now near the edge of the forest, Rachel dismounted Chestnut to scout out a place to camp for the night. She also kept her eye out for the road they were looking for; it was fairly easy to spot. She walked a short distance in, and then her heart sank. She had found the road but there was a large blockade where the newer road of Brenton had previously met up with the older road coming out of the forest. There were large boulders, fallen trees, and debris piled high; it looked as if it had been blocked for several years. She had never thought to ask if the road she had heard about was still in use. There was nothing she could do now except set up camp.

One thing was certainly true about the stories she had heard – this forest was ancient! The large, old pine trees stretched up into the moonlit night. She could feel something about this place that was nagging at her senses – a familiarity, a sense of déjà vu. It was a strange sensation.

"Campfire, supper, sleep. I can't do anything about this forsaken road until morning … but surely this can't be it. Maybe there's another way. Maybe I could go around … maybe … oh, hang it all!!" she cried as she slumped down in defeat.

Rachel sat there for some time, just allowing the tears to roll down her cheeks. Why hadn't she been better prepared for this journey? Here she was, so close and now with little to no hope of reaching her destination. She had been gone from home for days now, riding miles upon miles alone. She wondered how Jon was doing. Was her trip a complete waste? The tears felt hot on her cheeks, frustration bringing the sting of their heat. Finally, Chestnut must have figured she had done enough sulking. He quietly walked up behind her and with his nose gave her a shove. Totally not expecting that, Rachel lurched forward and face-planted in a cluster of valerian plants. Realizing how utterly foolish she must look, all she could do was laugh.

With a deep sigh, she got herself up and brushed the dirt and plant pieces from the front of her tunic and leggings. She shot a wicked glance at Chestnut. He merely gave a nicker and stared back. Rachel apologized for feeling sorry for herself and for her crying and began to remove her gear from Chestnut's saddle. She set about collecting firewood and again heard that familiar little voice in her head.

[*So close ... I can feel you ... can you feel me?*] The voice sent a chill up Rachel's spine.

"That's it, conscience. Way to freak me out. Yes, I know. We're so close to Geerda but I have no idea how to go the rest of the way! And what do you mean you can *feel* me? Of course, you can feel me. You are me! Chestnut, I'm sorry, I think I've lost my mind. Here I am having a conversation with my own conscience!" she proclaimed with her hands running through her hair as she took down her braid.

With a yawn and a shake of her head, she decided it was all just too much for her to deal with tonight; it was time to get some sleep. She would start fresh in the morning. Tomorrow's decision would be to find a way or make her way back home. She prayed her journey wouldn't be over this quickly.

TRAVEL DAY SIX

A chill swept over Rachel as she woke. Waking up on the ground outside after the fire had gone out was not quite as nice as waking up at the cottage all snuggled in that fabulous quilt. Rachel wondered why those couldn't be gifts to travelers when they left the fireplace clean. She desperately wished she had that quilt with her now as she shivered under her thin blanket. Rachel forced herself to get up and re-braid her tangled hair as best as she could. She gathered a few small pieces of wood to stoke the embers of her fire. She would have some muffin-like cakes she bought in Brenton and warm up before searching for a new route into the forest. She only had one option, south.

She made a deal with Chestnut. "If a way through doesn't present itself by nightfall we'll have to turn back. How's that sound to you?" She felt a little silly speaking to Chestnut as if he understood but was satisfied when he flicked his head, surely agreeing with her.

Even still, doubts crept into her heart. Maybe the stories of elves helping to heal people were old stories. Maybe no one had actually seen them for as long as that road appeared to have been blocked. Could it really be the only safe entrance into the forest? Rachel hoped for an answer, not just any answer, but one that showed her a passageway!

For nearly a mile, Rachel led Chestnut. She didn't need to be riding him at this point; it was easier to poke her way into little areas that hinted at a possible path. None of them had panned out so far, but she kept going. The trees and underbrush were incredibly dense. After another mile or so, a familiar scent tickled her nose – some sort of oatmeal or sweet bread. She looked up from the ground she had been diligently searching and spotted a small, stone house a short distance from where she stood. It had a thatched roof and a chimney with a wisp of smoke swirling from its top. There was a welcoming little path lined with flowers that lead to the front door. Rachel decided to get a closer look. She tied Chestnut to a nearby tree so he wouldn't follow. She crept up quietly. She wasn't close enough to peer into a window but, if she worked up enough courage, that was her goal.

She positioned herself just to the south of the house and suddenly heard a surprised, "Hullo!" She popped up from her crouched position with an equally surprised look on her face. She was staring at a short, slightly portly man with a bushy, black beard. The man was holding a large bowl of freshly picked berries.

"I'm so sorry. It's just that I ... well ... I'm not going to hurt you or anything. I'm lost," she rambled at the man who, in turn, just stared back. There was no change to his expression as he popped one of the berries into his mouth.

"OK, well, let's get you unlost then," he mumbled and continued to speak calmly around the ripe fruit. "Where were you heading, and where did it go wrong?"

Rachel blinked a couple times and laughed quietly. The man had turned toward the path, picked a few more berries, and motioned over his shoulder for her to follow. When they went into the house, he introduced himself as Forrin, introduced her to his wife and four small (very small) children. Forrin was no taller than Rachel and his petite wife, Brondi, may have been five feet tall if she stood on her tip-toes. They were getting ready to eat some oat scones with berries and fresh honeycomb. The oldest child,

Ranek, brought an extra chair to the table and nodded his head to her with a confident smile. He was very much a little gentleman of maybe ten years old with shiny, black hair like his father. Two girls, Ori and Gim, the spitting image of their mother, sat down as well as the youngest son, Darnen. Rachel was handed a scone and small bowl of berries with honey. How could she resist?

The inside of the home was cozy, just as Rachel would expect. The dining room table and chairs were smaller than she was used to. Rachel was quite comfortable but anyone taller would have felt as if their knees were trying to meet up with their ears. There was a great deal to look at in the quaint, little house. Bookshelves were overflowing with tomes of various sizes and colorful bindings. The mantle over the neatly laid brick fireplace was laden with carved wooden figurines and candles of varying sizes. Around the fire were two overstuffed chairs that had seen many years of use. There were four smaller versions of the same comfortable seats, all in different shades of deep red material. Everyone had their own chair.

The children all sat wide-eyed, looking at Rachel as if she were about to tell a great tale. Brondi gave them each a motherly stare, silently admonishing them for their lack of manners. When it came time to tell them 'where she was heading and where it went wrong', as Forrin had put it, she hesitated. Sharing knowing glances, Forrin and Brondi almost blurted out at the same time, "Geerda, huh?" and then laughed to each other.

Rachel's eyes widened and she sat bolt upright, then quickly tried to disguise her reaction.

"It's OK now. We aren't no spies or friendly with that poor excuse of a king, and we reckon neither are you. People don't just come this way. They are either our kin or lookin' for Geerda."

Interesting, Rachel thought. *More people, who were not fans of the king. This is becoming quite common.*

Rachel felt she could trust this couple and she relaxed. She admitted that, yes, she was looking for Geerda, but had come to the blocked road and was losing hope. With another scoop of berries spooned into her bowl by Brondi, Rachel listened as they told her about an alternate route.

They told her that if she continued south around the base of Mt. Spire and knew just what to look for, she would find the way in. "The Twin Tree will show you the way," said Forrin with a wink. Rachel gave him a puzzled frown, so he continued.

"Back nearly twenty years ago, there was some trouble in the elven village. Wouldn't you say, missus?" He looked at Brondi for confirmation then back at Rachel. "Something to do with King Desmond and his cousin. Anyway, you don't have time for all the details, but shortly after that, King Stephan ordered that old road to be blocked for good. Well, some of those magical elves still needed a way out of that old forest so they made a new path. Not many know of it, mind you, but it's marked with a tree planted by their chief. It split as it grew. Darn thing looks like two trees sprouted up from one trunk! Thus, the name. You find that, you'll find your path. But you got to go almost clear in a circle around it. They don't want it obvious. Not just anyone is welcome in there, you know."

Rachel's heart leapt with joy and a tad bit from apprehension; here was the answer she had hoped for. After a short discussion of some additional helpful information, the cute little family bid her farewell and wished Rachel luck. She had tried to pay full attention but she was anxious to get back on the road. Even they had mentioned that it was a full day's ride, so she knew she had better get going. She went back for Chestnut, who could sense her renewed joy, and off they went at a gallop.

The ground switched from sandy gravel to heavier rock but Chestnut was surefooted and got them through fairly easily. It felt as if they had been going all day, as it tends to when you are excited about something. Time dragged on and on. Rachel held a hand up to shield her eyes; the sky was bright but wouldn't be for long. She noticed some ominous clouds rolling in from the southeast. Based on the position of the sun, it was only midafternoon. She knew they had better stop for a short rest.

There was a small trickle of a waterfall coming off a low crag in the mountain. Rachel dismounted to obtain the ice-cold trickle in her cupped hands. She drank in as much as she could before refilling her water pouch. She offered the makeshift bowl of her palms to Chestnut. His soft muzzle tickled her fingers as he drank. The water refreshed them both.

"We better get to that tree and find a place with some shelter, fast! It looks like we're in for quite a storm," she exclaimed to Chestnut as she got back in the saddle to continue on. Rachel leaned back for her pack and pulled out a heavier shawl with a hood just in time. The rain made it to them before they had made it to the tree. They trudged on for at least two more hours in the rain. Her eyes continually scanned the area for a cave or grouping of trees they could huddle under but she saw nothing. She urged Chestnut on. The water began to come down from the sky as if it were angry about having to fall, splatting against and stinging Rachel's face as it hit. She *usually* didn't mind the rain, but she *usually* wasn't out in it, with no chance to escape its drenching.

Finally, there was a small path that led to an overhang tall enough for Chestnut and Rachel to stand under. The rain came cascading down the ledge from above. Rachel slid out of the saddle. Her boots splashed down in a shallow puddle. She pulled Chestnut's reigns and encouraged him in. It wasn't a cave but went farther back than she first thought. The sky grew dark with more menacing clouds and Rachel removed her shawl and wrung out the end of her braid. She got a small towel out and wiped Chestnut down. *At least we're under cover now. Maybe I can start a fire,* she thought. She didn't want to give up for the day but there didn't seem to be much else to do. There may only have been a couple more hours of daylight if the storm hadn't come, so it didn't completely deflate her mood. Surprise took over as she searched the area for some dry kindling and wood. She found enough to confirm the suspicions that she was not the first person to use this shelter. She was grateful for it.

After the fire got going, her shawl was hung near its warmth to dry. The rest of Rachel's clothes had been mostly covered, so she didn't have to worry about the chill from being wet. Her boots were damp, but that was to be expected.

She set out her bedroll and got out an apple for Chestnut. She felt he deserved it as she had worked him hard that day. Smoked fish and a fruit she was not very familiar with were on the evening menu. She had seen these bright orange fruits at the markets near Brimley but had never tried one prior to this trip. When the lady selling them in Brenton had given her a small sample, she had to buy more than one! They looked similar to an apple, had the juicy snap of a pear, and the flavor hinted at something she had not recognized. It was sweet and tart at the same time – a sharp, bold flavor soothed by a sweet, smooth aftertaste that left her mouth watering. She savored the flavor as long as she could.

The rain, mixed with the wind coming from the east, continued to thrash the leaves and needles on the surrounding trees. Rachel was relieved to be under this rock formation as the wind caused the temperature to drop. Dry as she was, she shivered from the damp air around them. She stood near Chestnut, and prepared to remove the saddle. Luckily, she had a grip on the reins as a flash of lightning spooked him and then a peel of thunder nearly caused him to bolt. She got the saddle off and tied him to a root at the side of the overhang that looked secure.

Stroking his forehead and neck calmed him down. After a short time, the wind died down and the clouds lightened. It was still raining but the severity of the storm had mellowed. Even though it was much cooler now, the feeling in the air was considerably calmer. Daylight was waning and Rachel decided to try to get some sleep. Her boots were placed neatly beside her shawl to take advantage of the fire's warmth while she slept. Thoughts of the Twin Tree swirled in her mind as she drifted off.

TRAVEL DAY SEVEN

Rachel had fallen asleep quickly the night before, not realizing at the time just how tired she was. She obviously needed the rest. Sunlight streamed into the side of the overhang. It was nearly nine in the morning. Taking a few deep breaths of this fresh, after-the-storm air, she craned her neck to spot Chestnut. Still tied to the root he had been tied to the night before, his gaze suggested that he would like to be untied to do some grazing. She stood up quickly, got her boots on (they were dry and warm), and granted him his wish. She snuck off to the shadowed side of their camp, wishing she still had access to the bathing room in the cottage.

How that cottage spoiled me. She laughed to herself. As Rachel came back around, she gathered her things and got them packed back onto Chestnut, leading him back out to the road.

They walked no more than fifty paces when she stepped wrong on a rock and stumbled forward. Unable to stop her forward momentum, she cursed as her knees hit the ground with a sickening crunch. Even if it was only in front of a horse, it was still embarrassing. She winced as she stood up facing the mountain, brushing off her knees. Her mouth fell open and she remained motionless for a good minute. There in front of her was a large tree ... with one base and two trunks climbing twenty feet above her head.

How could people miss this? OK, maybe if they weren't looking for it, she mused. Since the shared base of the trunk went up less than a foot before splitting, most people probably just didn't think about it. Rachel did a little jump with a faint squeal of excitement as she clapped her palm on Chestnut's neck.

"There it is ... our way through," she whispered to Chestnut as she stopped her little dance, reminded of the pain in her knees.

Remembering what Forrin and Brondi had told her about finding the path, Rachel led Chestnut in a clockwise circle around the trunk (or trunks) of the Twin Tree. The rock of the mountain closed in around them like a narrow tunnel with no roof. If a person did not know that it continued on, they would most likely turn back, as it appeared to be a dead-end. Soon they found themselves coming back around counter-clockwise almost from where they had begun. It was a good thing too; it was beginning to feel like a tight squeeze for her and Chestnut.

As the tunnel opened up before them, a well-groomed, gravel path was exposed. It was approximately six to eight feet wide, with trees (surely as old as the world itself) all around. There was a definite beauty to the forest that thickened as they progressed. An odd feeling surrounded them in this unfamiliar terrain.

Rachel had been in several wooded areas, mostly pine forests, but these trees were unlike any she had ever seen. The bark was dark and rough, covered with knots and vivid, green moss. The trunks were wide, gnarled, and twisting with each protruding branch. The leaves were a light green at the base then darkened toward the rounded edges to a deep plum color. They made a faint rustling noise as a breeze came through. The further in they went, the darker it became as the road narrowed and the trees crowded in around them. Thick ferns were covering the ground between the trees along with what appeared to be berry bushes dotted throughout.

Rachel knew better than to stray from the path, but those bushes had a light salmon-colored berry the size of a baby's fist; she really thought they were tempting her. Forrin and Brondi had warned her about straying from the path. There were rumors of the path changing course once you left it, making it nearly impossible to find your way back.

[*Raiza!*] She heard in her thoughts.

"Yes, yes, conscience … I know. I'm staying on the path," she sighed as she audibly responded to the voice in her head. She hadn't meant to say it quite so loudly though. The few sounds of the forest that had been buzzing around her now suddenly stopped. The silence was eerie. Chestnut noticed it and came to a halt as well. After a moment, the awkward silence was replaced by the hushed forest sounds once again. Chestnut resumed his prior pace.

Rachel thought back to all the stories she had heard about this place as a child and on her travels so far. They all spoke of dark magic, foul creatures, ghosts and wild animals. She wasn't sure why, but she could feel the magic here. It didn't feel dark or evil; it felt strangely familiar. It felt comforting.

Just as she was feeling like she could get through this place with no troubles, the hair on the back of her neck stood on end and chills ran throughout her body. Something was not right!

Maybe now is a good time to get back on Chestnut, she advised herself. If something was lurking in the shadows, it would be a much faster escape on hoof than on foot. She steadied the horse and got herself situated in the saddle.

Peering through the trees became more and more difficult; she could barely see fifteen feet in front of her. A strange clicking noise to her left made both she and Chestnut do a little jump. Farther down the path, it sounded again, this time to her right. Then more clicking and scratching sounds began to echo from every direction. She looked up to the sky to see if there would be some sort of creature coming at her from the treetops but saw nothing. She whirled around in the saddle from left to right.

She urged Chestnut farther and farther into this unknown. The clicking noises continued but at least the scratching noises had diminished as they rounded a sharp turn to their left to avoid a mound in the soil. It stood four feet tall and five to six feet wide and seemed to come out of nowhere. Once they were around it, Rachel could see a small entrance as if it was some creature's den. She watched the opening carefully. It was partially covered with gnarled roots and draping vines. The utter darkness from within gave her a sinking feeling.

Chestnut stopped suddenly, and Rachel's eyes shot back to the path in front of them. What she saw forced her to draw in a sharp breath. The clicking had all but stopped, and the air was quiet. There, blocking their path, were dozens of small creatures like no other Rachel had ever seen or could have imagined. She could not help the soft 'aaaww' sound that escaped her, as you might make when seeing a basket of baby animals. She giggled and clapped her hand over her mouth when the largest one (only a mere ten inches tall) clicked his tongue and nodded in her direction.

Cute as they were, Rachel wasn't sure how to react to these little beings. Most of them were around eight inches tall with a sort of fur or more like a combination of hair and moss that went from their heads down their chests and backs, into a swooping furry tail. Their pale green eyes were enormous and the round pupils nearly swallowed the color around them, lending even more to their cuteness. Otherwise, they looked like tiny people. They stood on two legs, had little hands with a thumb and three long fingers. Some held staffs or tiny curved knives.

None of them seemed to be hostile but stood their ground and would not let Chestnut go past. Rachel decided to try communication, or at least something to get them to step aside. As she slowly slid off Chestnut's back, the creatures swarmed her legs and she wondered if she had made the wrong decision. She soon realized they were all just touching her legs and some even patting or reaching around her ankle in a sideways hug. She smiled down at them in confusion and was taken aback when most of them smiled back up at her. They had surprisingly straight, white, feline-like teeth. One by one, after a quick hand gesture from their leader, they lowered their staffs and knives to Rachel's delight.

They clicked at each other, and she realized they were the reason for her earlier panic. Rachel found it funny how the unknown can terrify people when it is nothing to be frightened of. Certainly these beings were the friendly sort.

Chestnut stepped to the opposite side of the road to graze and Rachel got her satchel of food off his saddle. Now was as good a time as any for a quick snack. Maybe she could offer something to these new friends as a kind gesture. She had to step carefully and slowly to avoid stepping on the tiny, furry people, and found a log to sit on. Several of the creatures climbed up next to her or on her. They appeared to be very curious as to what was in her satchel.

She showed them a few items as she brought them out. First, she drew some cheese from the satchel; they were unimpressed. Next, she produced some small, cracker-like pieces of flat bread; still not impressed. When the last of her bright orange fruits came out, the group went into an excited frenzy, dancing from one tiptoe to the other and back again.

Obviously, they were familiar with this fruit. Their eyes grew even wider than Rachel thought possible. She was skeptical that one fruit would be enough to share, but was afraid of the repercussions if she didn't at least try. She carefully cut the fruit in half, then in half again, and again, and kept cutting until there were several tiny pieces.

Starting with what she thought was their chief, she rose to pass out the tiny chunks and was touched that the younger looking beings would pass their piece to the elders first. When there were several creatures left but no more fruit pieces, Rachel held out her arms apologetically. She then noticed that none of them had started eating yet. Those with larger chunks began to break them to share with the others who had none. Rachel sat back down and by the time she was settled, every one of them had at least a small piece of fruit in his or her hand. Then they all began to purr, or something similar to a purr, as they began to eat. It was quite possibly the cutest thing Rachel had ever witnessed.

The new friends finished their fruit, licking their tiny fingers of every drop of the sweet juices, and Rachel finished her cheese and flat bread. The apparent leader made a small noise similar to a whistle and waved his hand toward the back of the little crowd. The group made way for one of their own to hobble her way through (at least it looked like a girl to Rachel; it was hard to tell the gender of these critters). She slowly started to climb up Rachel's leg, but as she did, Rachel could tell something made it difficult for her. Rachel bent over and offered her hand to help the injured girl the rest of the way. She grabbed onto Rachel's thumb to steady herself and blinked up at Rachel with a tear in her eye.

Rachel carefully helped her sit down on her right thigh as the chief pointed out to Rachel the gash on the girl's leg and heel. Rachel couldn't think of anything she had in her limited supplies that would help the poor thing but she examined the wound anyway. The cut went from the back of her knee, diagonally across her calf, and ended just under her ankle bone at the back of her heel. It looked infected and very painful.

The only thing Rachel could think to do was to wash and bandage it. She used some of the water from the waterfall she and Chestnut had been at and wrapped the wound with a small piece of the sleeve of her tunic. The chief looked on in confusion and seemed to be frustrated by her actions. Rachel spoke soothingly to the girl as she worked and, in turn, the girl seemed to be reassuring the chief that it was helping. Rachel couldn't really tell, but if body language meant the same thing with these tiny beings as it did with humans, that would be her best guess.

Once the bandage was in place, the girl snuggled up to Rachel's side and began to purr again. Rachel wasn't sure if petting her would be appropriate, but she couldn't help it. She began to gently stroke the rough fur on the top of the girl's head. The girl flashed a grin that stretched the whole width of her face; that was a good enough sign for Rachel.

Rachel wasn't sure how long they had been in this part of the forest but she felt comfortably at peace and completely anxious all at once. How that was possible, she didn't know. The forest itself had a calming effect on Rachel that she couldn't explain. It worried her that she didn't know exactly where she was going or how much farther she needed to go. How would she know if she was even going in the right direction? She only knew that she had better keep going if she ever hoped to reach Geerda.

Most of the creatures had left; there were only five of them remaining. The girl still cuddled against her, the chief sat upon her boot leaning on her shin, two that looked like males curled up on the log next to her, and another (possibly female) propped against Rachel's right leg. Rachel stirred gently and gave all but the chief a little pet, then carefully set the injured girl on the ground next to him. They figured out what was going on and headed back toward the mound with contented clicks and smiles.

"How adorable were they, Chestnut?" He brought his head up from grazing to acknowledge her as she strapped her satchel back onto his back. She felt like walking for a while to stretch out her muscles. As they walked, they heard other noises: birds, leaves rustling, small animal chatter, but nothing that was unsettling. Rachel figured she would at least try not to be such a chicken. After all, the source of the scary, clicking noises turned out to be some of the sweetest folks she had ever come across.

After a few more hours at a brisk pace, Rachel mounted Chestnut again, and was certainly glad she did. Out of the corner of her eye she saw something move. It was farther into the trees, so she couldn't make out what it was, but it was large and if she needed a quick get-away at least she was ready.

She tried to keep Chestnut steady as she craned her neck to peer through the foliage; she still could not see what seemed to be tracking them. There was something there, but what or whom she could not say. The being was up a slope and deeper into the trees. As soon as she thought she could focus on it, it would vanish from her vision. Suddenly, the feeling of the presence was gone, with no further sightings. She could hear more clicking sounds in the distance. This time it brought her comfort. She smiled and continued on.

"There must be hundreds of those creatures in these woods," she said quietly to herself.

Darkness was settling over the forest and the path began to be more difficult to see. Rachel felt herself drifting off and had a difficult time keeping her eyes open and focused on the path ahead for the next hour. She shook off her drowsiness enough to dismount and find a place to camp for the evening.

Off to the right some twenty feet, there was a tree bent so close to the ground that it made a natural tent out of the hanging branches. This would provide shelter and help to hide her from the path in case anything else was watching her. She tied Chestnut behind the shelter of a massive tree trunk nearby and began to remove the gear from his back. She felt it was best not to have a fire tonight, but sat comfortably in her 'tent' with a small supper and then lay down for the evening. She could barely make out the blue tones of the sky through her leafy ceiling.

She wondered how far she still had to travel to find the people who held her brother's future in their hands. It mattered very little to her at this point. She would go as far as she needed.

Merri Gammage

TRAVEL DAY EIGHT

A quiet calm blanketed the forest as Rachel's eyes opened. She rubbed her face and stretched out. She could see Chestnut at the side of the tree with his head down, pawing at the ground. She yawned as she sat up and began to get dressed. She would continue the same path today hoping for the best.

Rachel wasn't sure what the weather would bring, but it was dry so far, with a mild temperature, and that was good enough. With her gear packed and her mind clear, she and Chestnut got back on the road. As she glanced around, she realized the path, which had been to the left of the tree when she fell asleep, was now to the right. So Forrin and Brondi's suspicions had been warranted. She found it very strange. She could see the overcast sky through the tree tops and hoped that they were still heading west. Trusting her gut was her only option.

The road wove in a gentle, snake-like pattern, back and forth through the gnarled trees. Every now and then, there would be a smaller road that branched off to one side or the other, but Rachel stayed true to the main road. She felt relaxed and hopeful. She kept an eye on her surroundings as they pressed on to make sure they were safe, never seeing anything to be concerned about.

The steady crunch of Chestnut's hooves on the gravelly path filled Rachel's ears. She allowed herself to close her eyes and lean back in the saddle. How did this forest have such a calming effect on her? She wondered how all the rumors of horrific happenings got started. The path changing had been unsettling, but for some reason it hadn't been as scary as she thought it might be. She was completely at peace.

While her eyes were still closed, she extended her arms out to her sides to shake them out, momentarily releasing the reins. That turned out to be a mistake! Something spooked Chestnut. He jolted forward, and then reared up with a loud whinny. Rachel went to the ground with a painful thud before she could even grasp what was happening. The wind was knocked from her lungs. Her head smacked the ground as she fell from her mount. Chestnut turned and darted down the road in the direction from which they had come. Rachel momentarily saw the tops of the trees becoming grey and fuzzy as they faded from her vision. She blacked out.

The subtle hint of smoke tickled Rachel's nostrils as she began to wake up, but she had a hard time opening her eyes. Her head felt like it weighed one hundred pounds and throbbed with a pain so great it made her ill. She tried to roll to the side as her stomach lurched, but the pain in her hips and back stopped her.

What happened? She tried to remember. Slowly and with much effort, she was able to blink open her eyes. The surroundings were mostly blurred. She saw a shadowy figure and felt a warm hand on her forehead, then heard a man's voice telling her to relax and that she was safe. Her mind began to race. Against the advice of the shadowy figure, she tried to sit up. He gently held her shoulders.

"Not so fast. Give yourself some time. You had quite a fall."

That's right. She remembered now. She had been thrown from Chestnut's back. *Chestnut! Where had he gone?* She choked out the name, broken sounding and barely audible.

The man guessed that she was asking about the horse. He told her he was unable to catch up to him on foot and had to return to make sure she was OK. "I'm not sure what spooked him. Something, or someone, was stalking you. I couldn't risk leaving you here alone to find out what it was."

Rachel's eyes were beginning to open a bit easier now. She blinked several times to clear them as she brought her hand up to feel the knot at the back of her head. She grimaced as she touched the tender lump. Her vision was clearing.

There in front of her was a man of her age. He had rich brown hair just long enough for his bangs to sweep in front of his clear, blue eyes as he bent down to look into hers. He was well built, and Rachel guessed he was six feet tall. She thought he was exceptionally good looking. She quickly averted her gaze and began to fiddle with the end of her braid.

The action caused the man to study her as if reminded of someone else he knew. He offered to help Rachel sit up and she accepted, only to shy away from his touch in embarrassment. *Who is he? Why is he here? Where are we?* Questions began to stack up in Rachel's mind as she made herself as comfortable as she could.

She was extremely sore. She looked up to the sky to get her bearings. "How long have I been unconscious?"

The man shrugged his shoulders. "About half an hour or so?" He brought her a cup of steaming liquid that smelled like pepper. "Drink this. It will take much of your pain away within minutes. It is something my grandmother taught me how to make," he explained.

Rachel wondered why she trusted this man as she began to drink. She felt as if she could tell him anything. Not caring one bit for the flavor, she gulped the hot liquid as quickly as she could, burping afterward. She turned her face away with flushed cheeks. *Way to go Rachel. Impress him with that little gem.*

[*It's nothing to be embarrassed about,*] her conscience butted in. At this, she rolled her eyes.

When the man took the cup from her and saw her eyes roll, he touched her shoulder. "Are you OK?"

"Yes, sorry, my mind is just all over the place, I feel like I have so many questions …" she trailed off as she looked down at her hands.

"Ask away," he prompted with a warm smile.

That smile could surely melt the top of Mt. Spire! But it had a different effect on Rachel than she expected it to. She began to wonder why she had no butterflies or stirring feelings for this near perfect specimen in her presence. She took a deep breath, noticed it didn't hurt nearly as badly as it had, and started asking questions. "What is your name?"

"Well, my name is Rainor, I live near here, and lucky for you, I was out looking for ..." he stopped himself mid-sentence when his facial expression changed, a sudden flash of recognition evident in his expression.

"Yes? You were looking for what?" Rachel prompted him to finish.

"Not 'what'. 'Whom'," he said quietly, looking at her intently.

[*Raiza?*] Her conscience seemed to whisper in her mind, then again louder, [*Raiza, could it really be?*]

Rachel looked around as if her conscience had somehow left her body and was someone else trying to get her attention. It had never sounded like this before. She was suddenly confused and worried that she had hit her head harder than she thought. Her hands went up to her temples and she tightly closed her eyes.

Rainor put his hands over hers. They were warm and gentle, so she allowed them to stay there.

[*Raiza, it's OK, don't be afraid. It's me, Rainor. It's my voice you are hearing. I have been searching for you! I have been trying to make contact with you for years, dear sister. Why have you not responded? Can you respond, Raiza? Do you know who I am? Or even who you are?*]

"Wait … WHAT?" Rachel gasped as her eyes flew open, and she scrambled to her feet. She backed away a few steps, turned her back to Rainor, and shook her head in disbelief. When she turned back over her shoulder, she pointed at him with a shaky finger. She was barely able to get her breath and demanded, "Do that again!" then in a softer tone asked. "But … slower please." She was terribly confused and felt suddenly vulnerable.

He now knew she was his sister, but wasn't quite sure why she seemed to have no knowledge of him or how to mind-speak like he had been able to do since birth. Gently, slowly, he spoke to her mind again.

[*It seems that I am able to hear some of your thoughts, and I can speak to you without vocalizing. Are you not able to do this, with me?*]

Rachel's breathing sped up as she turned to completely face Rainor again, mouth hung open in awe. She slowly shook her head side to side, not having a clue how to return the answer to his question.

"Please, sit," he motioned to a nearby log.

She slowly sat back down, never taking her eyes off of him (but she did manage to close her mouth). "Did you call me 'sister'?" she eventually blurted out.

"Yes, I wasn't sure at first. You look different than I had imagined you would. But as I spoke to you, I could feel it. I had to try one more time, mentally, to verify it … but I heard, or felt, your embarrassment after you drank the pain remedy and … well … burped…" He didn't want to further embarrass her so he stopped there.

She rubbed her face with both hands and let out a small laugh. This was all such a shock. "I have a brother?" she asked quietly. *A hot one … that must be why no butterflies. That's a relief!*

Without even thinking, Rainor laughed at her thought (that he could 'hear'). He would have to try and teach her how to block private thoughts. She shot her eyes up to meet his and knew right away he had heard that very thought. She groaned and buried her face in her hands yet again.

Rainor sat next to her. "Don't worry. It's OK." He now had several questions flooding his mind and knew there was much to discuss with his sister. "Raiza, I should probably begin by finding out how you came to be in Morgan Forest. Were you coming in search of me?" Rainor asked with hope-filled eyes.

"Um, it's Rachel ... my name. I mean ... that's what I go by. But how did you know to call me Raiza? That is what I called myself as a toddler. I had trouble saying Rachel so it came out as Raiza ... and no, until a moment ago, I did not know that you existed. I'm sorry. I came looking for help for my foster brother, Jon. He's very ill and in need of a healer," Rachel looked at him with pleading eyes and did not hesitate to hide her motives for her journey. It was so easy to communicate with him.

Rainor's hope that she was there for the same purpose he had been, in searching for her, vanished. It didn't matter though. She was there.

"Actually, your given name is Raiza. That's how I knew to call you that. I didn't know you went by anything else. We're twins, Raiza … not just siblings, but twins." He was trying not to overwhelm her, but it was not working as he continued to tell her more. "Um, we're also half human and half elf. Our mother is an elf and our father was human. And one more thing I should probably tell you. I saw you … with the bushkins," (the little creatures Rachel, or Raiza, had fallen in love with the prior day).

"So, you were the one I could sense following us?" she asked him.

"No, it wasn't me. I did see you before you saw me though. I hadn't quite found a way to approach you yet. The bushkins told me, before you met them, that they could sense you were a healer. So, I was going to watch you from a distance to see if it was true. When you could do no more than clean and dress Itsi's leg, I figured you were just some lost human … and nothing more." As he told her this, his face twisted in confusion.

She sighed and snorted back "That's really all I am … or was … before your news that I am half elf!" She smiled sheepishly at him then asked, "Can you tell me more about the bushkins?"

"They only approach elves, usually, or children. Normally they try to scare people out of the forest, clicking as they herd them to the nearest forest exit," he laughed a bit when he continued. "You should have seen how frustrated the elder, Otni, had been when you didn't know your own talent. You are a healer, Raiz ... er ... Rachel. Sorry, but you don't seem to have been raised with any of the knowledge about who you are. All of the elves have a talent, or a gift. I have a talent for languages, any kind – with humans, elves, animals – all by making eye contact. I can only communicate truth and those communicating with me are forced to do the same."

That part explained how Rachel had wanted to tell him everything and trust in him so easily. "I have been well hidden in Geerda most of my life. The time for me to meet back up with you, to fulfil our destiny, is nearly two years overdue. If things had gone as they should have, we would have been reunited on our eighteenth birthday and training would have been done for both of us as we matured. Looks like I will have to give you a crash course. We only have another year before things may be too late." With that, he stood up, reached for her hand to help her up, and recommended that they get to Geerda. He would explain more as they walked.

Rachel was overwhelmed. She tried to take everything in as Rainor spoke. He walked at a quick pace with his long legs and held himself straight and tall, looking every bit like a prince or born leader. It made Rachel feel somewhat smaller and more insignificant than she normally did. She practically had to trot to keep up with him now.

At one point, he glanced to his side to make sure she understood everything, and noticed the difference in their strides. He paused to let her catch up and catch her breath then continued at a slower pace.

"I have grown up in Geerda. Our mother (Eleese), grandfather and grandmother (Therik and Lin) are there too. I lived with another family while I grew up though. The elves wanted King Stephan to think Eleese's child had perished, but I would rather allow Eleese to finish that story."

Rainor also shared that Rachel had been sent with trusted human friends of Eleese after they were born. She was to be raised in Brimley with all the knowledge of her heritage, trained in her healing abilities, and combat skills.

At this point, Rachel stopped Rainor. "Are the Mills the trusted human friends you mentioned?"

He shook his head "They are not, I'm not sure what the other family's name was, but we had lost contact with them back when you and I were toddlers."

"I wonder what happened to them ..." Rachel said quietly.

"Me too ..." Rainor replied just as quietly.

After a brief moment of silence, they began to walk again and Rachel came up with more questions. "You know, as we are walking through here, I notice it's not nearly as scary as all the stories I've grown up hearing. Why are people so afraid to come here? Are there really dangerous creatures and ghosts and things?"

Rainor scrunched his face in thought. "There are only a couple of creatures that could really do anyone any harm. They usually stay close to the north or south shores. I think that they might be responsible for the sightings by the old road before it was closed. One of them is a large, nocturnal, bird-like creature called a ravat. They have matte black feathers, haunting white eyes, and make an eerie sound while they are mating," he laughed nervously. He had never seen one but had heard their cry. "They have been known to attack when people got too close to their nests. Since it was most likely at night when they were seen, they could be pretty scary to behold.

"The other creature, a jackoyt, is similar to a wild dog or coyote, but larger. They have light grey or white fur, small yellow eyes, and a mouth full of sharp fangs, almost too many for it to close its lips," Rainor shuddered at this. "I saw some as a child. I couldn't bring myself to make eye contact, otherwise I would have been able to communicate with the foul things ... but who would want to?" he confessed. He shook his head to get the memory of it out of his mind. "I was in a tree when I spotted them. Otherwise I believe they would have killed me."

Rachel risked a quick glance around to make sure none of those horrid things were close by.

Rainor chuckled when he noticed her. "I assure you, you're safe. They usually only came out at night. Besides, most of the fears people had about the forest itself was probably based off rumors the friendly humans had helped to spread, along with the dwindling number of dwarves ... before they went into hiding."

"Dwarves? Really? I thought they were just a myth. You don't think that jackoyt was what had been stalking me earlier, do you?" Rachel asked with concern.

"No ... those beasts don't let up that easily. If it had been a jackoyt, you would be dead now. They don't let things go," Rainor assured her.

Rachel was relieved, but shuddered at the thought. "Do you think we could go back, for Chestnut? I hate the thought of him wandering alone. What about the path – how it changes? I experienced that this morning. It was quite odd. Will it have changed since he ran off?"

"I'm sure he'll find his way somewhere safe. I need to get you to Geerda as quickly as possible. We can have someone track him later. The path change is caused by a bit of ancient magic. But it's no surprise that you managed to find the correct direction. This forest knows you. The trees are continuously tended to by our kind and they take care of us. It could have been that whoever was stalking you was put off course by the shift overnight," Rainor gave Rachel a reassuring smile.

Now it was Rainor's turn to ask some questions of Rachel. "So, the Mills you mentioned earlier, are they the people who raised you? What are they like? What do they do? Will you go back to living with them after your journey? Do you live on your own? And who is Jon again? If he is ill, our mother can surely help. I think you'll love her,

Raiza. Sorry … Rachel. That will be difficult for me, at least for a little while."

Rachel couldn't help but laugh at how quickly he blurted out all those questions. He reminded her of herself when he did it. She tried to answer every question he had, and started by telling him about the Mills. "I thought they were my real parents my whole life, I have no memories from before I was three years old. I found out recently, that is about the same time they took me in. I'm not sure how it all happened. Jon is my little brother. Jack and Mavis had him when I was a teenager, he become ill a while back. The doctors were running tests on the family to see if they could determine a cause, or a cure, and that is when I found out they were not really my parents, that we're not blood related." As she relayed the information a few tears rolled down her cheek. Her throat hitched on a lump, now growing too large for her to continue.

Rainor turned apprehensively to hug her and was relieved when she welcomed the embrace. She felt safe and complete. She was the most complete she had ever felt in her whole life at that moment.

Her tears continued to flow, but more out of joy now than sorrow. They held each other, neither wanting to let go of their twin, now together after so long. When they both took in a deep breath and sighed at the same time, it made them both laugh. If anyone had seen them now, they would not have guessed the two had basically just met. The closeness, the special bond only twins can share, was impossible to deny.

The twins continued on and Rainor told Rachel there were only a few more miles until the edge of the forest. Geerda was just beyond that. Rachel's heart nearly skipped a beat. For the last hour of their walk, Rachel and Rainor continued to get to know one another. Rainor shared about his childhood. Rachel shared about her journey thus far. She lit up when she told him about the little family she met that told her of the Twin Tree.

"It was our grandfather who had planted that tree. The elves had molded it to grow that way, in honor of the two of us," Rainor told her.

"Wait a minute, they said the elf chief planted that tree. Maybe they had their story off?" she inquired.

"Nope, that's him. The chief is our grandfather," Rainor exclaimed proudly.

"So, are we some sort of royalty or something?"

"You have no idea, do you?" he said quietly, shaking his head. "You'll just have to get the whole story from Eleese, from *our mother,*" he told her with a knowing smile.

Rachel stopped; she stopped walking, stopped talking, and stopped everything except for breathing and blinking. "*Our mother,*" she repeated in a whisper as it all started to sink in.

The trees around her began to spin. Rainor turned back to see if she was OK. Rachel could see the concerned look on his face and gave him a weak smile.

"I never knew Mavis Mills wasn't my mother until just recently. When I found out the truth, I hadn't yet begun to wonder who my *real* mother could be! I was so focused on Jon and finding a way to help him. Now I will be meeting her ... today ... after meeting you – the twin brother I never knew I had – and grandparents ... you mentioned that they all still live in Geerda, right?" She looked at Rainor with raised eyebrows and continued on. "And what about my, I mean, *our* father? Do we have other family? Where are they? Oh, my. I need to sit." And that's just what she did, right down on the gravel pathway. Her hands were nervously fidgeting with her braid as soon as she landed.

Rainor plopped himself right beside her. This had been quite a day so far. After a moment, he glanced at her hands and said, "She does that too."

"Who? What?" Rachel asked.

"Our mother. The fidgeting," he said with a smile.

Rachel sighed, closed her eyes for a brief moment, and began to get up. "Let's get going," she told her brother. She held out a hand to help him up.

The sun was filtering through the trees a bit more as they began to emerge from the thick forest. Rachel could hear movement around them. She could not see anything or anyone as she glanced around.

Rainor pointed out the elven archers perched as guards in the trees at the forest's edge. "They have been up there for at least the last mile," he whispered to her. "Many of them are in training right now on how *not* to be detected."

Her eyes grew double their normal size when she realized just how many were up there. Not sure how to act or what to do, she gave a shy wave. Only one of the elves returned the gesture until he got a sharp elbow to the ribs by another on the same branch. Rachel turned away to hide a giggle.

As the trees cleared, and the path turned to their right, Rachel could tell they were facing north. When the path turned back almost completely the opposite direction, huts became visible ahead. Simple structures with thatched roofs and stone chimneys stood before her. Wooden doors that reminded Rachel of the bottom of a small boat completed the quaint little homes. There were gardens, and wells, and people ... well, elves. Rachel took a quick, deep breath as if she would scream but nothing followed.

Rainor took her hand and led her through the village. He pointed out various houses or people as they walked, waving to some curious onlookers along the way. Everyone's eyes were on them.

It wasn't completely uncomfortable for Rachel because of their friendly nature. She wondered how they would react when they found out who she was, or maybe they already knew. She tried to take it all in. Suddenly, Rainor had stopped and she hadn't. She bumped right into the man standing before them. She was embarrassed.

He had nearly the same color hair as Rainor and a similar build. *Not bad looking!* Rachel noted to herself.

Both young men smiled.

"Sage!" Rainor squeezed his friend's shoulder and introduced him to Rachel. "Sage, this is Rai ... Rachel. Rachel, Sage." He gave Rachel a sideways glance of apology for the name slip again. "Do you know where my mother is? Or my grandfather and grandmother? I must speak to them immediately!" he blurted out.

Sage looked at Rachel and back at Rainor with a knowing grin (but he really didn't know the situation). He had not made the connection that Rachel was Raiza. "You sly devil! Is this the human girl you've been meeting up with on your secret treks into the forest?"

"No ... NO! You've got it all wrong," Rainor abruptly corrected him, dropping Rachel's hand, and ran his own hand up through the side of his hair. "My mother? Therek? Lin? Where are they?"

"Calm down, brother. They are all in Therek's hut ... but tell me more later! Promise?" Sage laughed as he went on his way.

Rachel glanced back at him and noticed he was walking backwards to continue his curious gaze. He winked at her then trotted off. She turned to Rainor with a laugh, slightly blushing. "He thought … well, that we were … an item? Oh my goodness.

So, is there a human girl you are sneaking off with?" she asked as she lightly elbowed his ribs.

Rainor shook his head and rolled his eyes. "That is just the rumor in the village since I have been secretly venturing out in attempts to get information about you for over a year."

The twins continued down the main road then up a small hill to a large hut Rachel had not noticed before they were in front of it. It was tucked neatly on the side of the cliffs that stretched up as they reached west toward the sea. The hut was not much different from the others except for its size. It had two doors on the front, one at each end that made Rachel wonder if it was a dual dwelling.

They approached the door at the right. "This is where our grandfather and grandmother live. The other end is a meeting hall with a view of the sea and the sunset."

Rachel's face twisted in confusion as she looked to the door at the left. All she could see beyond it were more rocks. "I don't understand," she admitted.

"I'll show you after we go inside," and he motioned her in.

She stepped inside and immediately began to fiddle with the end of her braid.

After they entered the hut, Rachel deftly noticed it was much larger than it appeared from the outside. She took a seat on an L-shaped bench to her right. Rainor stepped around the wall to the left and into the sitting room to see his mother, Therek, and Lin, casually visiting by the large fireplace. It was set deep into the rock wall that separated the living quarters from the meeting hall. The fireplace went clear through to be enjoyed from either side. Therek was the first to notice Rainor.

"Rai! Come in, come in! We were discussing you just now. Could you sense it?" he asked with a smile. Rainor was very close to his grandfather. As he entered, he was also greeted by his grandmother's warm smile and his mother's embrace as she stood to greet him. He had been in the forest for three days, this time. It was nothing unusual for him these days.

"How long are you back for this time?" Eleese questioned him.

"That can wait, Mother. I have some wonderful news. I'd love to hear what you were all discussing," he said with a mock glare over his mother's head at Therek, "but that too can wait!"

Eleese laughed, "OK then, what is it?" Without warning, Rachel stepped into the entry of the sitting room.

There before her stood the most beautiful people Rachel had ever seen. Therek, her grandfather, looked to be in his fifties. Surely, he must be older, but his muscular frame and strong, broad shoulders did nothing to hint at his extended years. Rainor was built much like him but their coloring was very different. Therek's skin was a creamy ivory tone and his hair so light blond it was almost white. Although his eyes had very little color to them, a silvery light blue, they danced with warmth.

The two women in the room were shorter than Rachel. They each had the same figure and appeared very young. The older one must be her grandmother, Lin. She also had fair skin, blond hair, and light blue eyes. There was such grace to these women. Rachel felt herself shrink with insecurity in their presence (she wasn't as fit as either of them, nor did she feel as graceful).

There was only one person left. It had to be her. It had to be Rachel's mother, Eleese. She looked more like Therek than Lin, but in a much softer and smaller frame. She was staring back at Rachel with the same crystal-blue eyes as herself and Rainor. Eleese blinked only once then swept over to wrap her arms around Rachel as she whispered, "My Raiza, you're home."

Rachel returned the hug and breathed in her mother's scent for the first time in over fifteen years. *Fresh as the sea breeze on a sunny day. Warm. Welcoming.* Then she began to cry.

Rainor beamed with joy as Therek and Lin approached to join the family embrace.

It was just after mid-day now and even though they were not needed, introductions were officially made, and the hugging didn't stop for some time. Lin excused herself to the kitchen to gather some food for everyone. Rachel watched her as she worked side by side with the house help. While Rachel watched Lin, Eleese watched Rachel, taking in their similarities.

Rainor and Therek were now chatting about the prior discussion between his mother and grandparents. Rachel joined in the middle of Therek's explanation, "… her parents approached me the day after you left on this most recent trek into the forest. They wanted to persuade me that even though you and their daughter had not shared your inner names that I should nudge you in her direction." His view on the topic was written in the lines of disgust on his face. Therek was a firm believer of the old ways. Couples were only meant to be together when their inner names were discovered and not otherwise.

"You know, when your mother and father found each other, he had no inner name, being a human of course, but he knew your mother's," Therek gazed at the fire when he spoke of this, not sure Rainor had ever been told.

Rachel's head whipped around in curiosity. Lin, along with the help of a young girl, brought out some food and set it on the small table. It was set between the chairs that were arranged in a horseshoe pattern in the room. As they got seated, the girl excused herself and everyone selected their foods, Rainor gave a brief overview of what he had already shared with Rachel. Therek began to explain what he had been discussing with Rainor.

"Inner names are secret. They are discovered at birth when the babe, through unspoken communication, shares it with its parents. No one other than the mother and father knows the child's inner name until they meet the one other person they are destined to be with, to bond with in life. But there are some exceptions." At this statement he paused and looked between Rachel and Rainor, then continued. "I don't know your inner name but because you are twins, you share the same name. This is very rare and unique." Rainor sat smiling in understanding; he already knew all of this, but Rachel had a look of utter confusion on her face. It was not because what she was hearing was difficult to understand, just that she wondered if she knew her inner name. She had known her real name all of her life but had not been aware that was what it was. Could this inner name be something she knew without knowing as well?

Almost as if she could sense what Rachel was wondering, Lin said "Raiza dear? Do you know of your inner name?"

Without correcting her grandmother on the name she went by, she simply shook her head "I don't know whether I do or not."

Her grandparents smiled sympathetically with her.

"We can explore that later," Eleese offered.

Therek continued on by telling Rachel how her mother and father had met. "Eleese had been friends with a human named Desaree as a child. Desaree had grown up in Brenton with her father who would often venture into the forest for herbs. He was a general, and enjoyed cooking, if I remember correctly. He had been sent to the South, to Traither, to lead in some training when his daughter was sixteen. Because Desaree's mother had long since passed away, she went with her father and helped out in the kitchen of the military camp.

"After a full year's service, Desaree met and fell in love with Wilmond Arkens, then Prince of Brimley, though she was not aware of his status until after they had fallen in love. It was a quick courtship but a true love nonetheless. With blessings from both sides, the two united.

"Wilmond and Desaree had a son named William who became very ill as a child. Desaree tried to contact us for help, but was stopped; that is another tale for another time ..." Therek's words fell softly as he glanced at Eleese in sadness.

Her expressions gave little away, but Rachel could see the minute tightness around her mother's eyes. Therek sat silently for another moment as Rachel looked between the two. She was curious about the rest of the story, but she could sense there was much tension involved.

Eventually, he continued. "It was sometime later when Desaree decided to pay us a secret visit. She was now the queen and had to be discreet about coming to Geerda. She told us that she had sent for us, but heard nothing back, so she had to make the trip in person. We had not received any word from her but she gave us the sad news of her son passing, and of twin girls also lost; they had been born too soon. Lin assured her, after a healing session, that things would get better. She was soon on her way back to Brimley. Lin had discovered that Desaree was again pregnant but it was so early on, she did not tell her. After that, we sent out regular scouts to check up on our friend.

"After Prince Desmond was born, Eleese was old enough to join the scouting parties and volunteered to go to Brimley for occasional trips to watch over him. When there was news of King Wilmond passing, then shortly afterwards Desaree – leaving young Desmond the throne at only fifteen years of age – Eleese once again went to Brimley. She never revealed herself, but constantly watched out for Desmond. Over time, she felt her watchful eye was no longer needed, so she returned to Geerda. We occasionally sent other scouts and learned of

King Desmond's marriage. When we heard news that Desmond was taking secret outings with no guards, I feared something was wrong," Therek paused for a drink.

Rachel noticed Rainor was just as much on the edge of his seat as she was. *Has he not heard this story before?* She looked him in the eye as if to secretly ask him and got the answer in her thoughts.

[*I have not heard this much detail on this; it is almost as new to me as to you!*]

They both looked back to Therek to continue.

"I suppose you want to hear the rest?"

"YES!" the twins blurted out.

"I asked Eleese, now highly skilled in tracking and the same healing skills as her mother, to seek him out, to watch over him once again. He was a grown man of twenty-five years and surely able to take care of himself, but there seemed no reason for him to be going off alone as he had been. I felt we owed it to dear Desaree to watch over him. Three years Eleese watched him; three years she was undetected. Then she became careless one day and he discovered her." At this statement, he gave Eleese a wink.

She smirked and looked away.

"Over the next year they were nearly inseparable ..." he said while glancing back at Rachel and Rainor with sorrow in his eyes.

Rachel sat in silence for a moment. Everyone else in the room stared in her direction. They, of course, knew the rest of the story. When she realized all eyes were on her, she looked from one to the next, carefully trying to read their thoughts. Then something dawned on her in such a rush as if someone had dumped a bucket of cold water on her head. She leapt up and nearly shrieked out the question the rest of them knew the answer to.

"Are we the former king's children?" She could barely breathe. One by one, the others nodded the confirmation. Rachel melted back down to her seat with a dazed expression.

Rainor extended his arm around her shoulder. "Grandfather, would you continue? Or ..." Then he looked to his mother as if to ask if she would rather tell the rest.

Therek nodded toward Eleese to continue.

With a tense pause, but otherwise remaining completely poised, she continued. "We cared very deeply for one another. A forbidden love, but a true love. After all that time watching him, I realized that on some level I had loved him all along. He returned that love. One day, he spoke my inner name out loud, as if it were a cough or sneeze he could no longer contain. This was unheard of in prior elf-human relationships; it was something very special. I knew then, that man, that human man, was to be my bond."

Rachel asked Therek about the queen, "I remember you mentioning that Desmond had taken a queen?"

"Sadly, she passed during the labor of their first child; neither survived," Therek explained. "This was the cause of Desmond's lone outings. He had seen so much heartache and loss."

Lin spoke up now. "In my vision, so many years prior, when I had seen Desmond as an unborn baby, still in his mother's womb, I had seen the future moment of Eleese and Desmond when he had blurted out her inner name. I had not been confident in my own vision, not having had any prior visions, and did not want to influence anyone. So, I kept it a secret."

Therek, Eleese, and Lin continued to share small details to the story as Rachel and Rainor listened intently. Some of the details were new to Rainor, but most he already knew. Somehow, having Rachel there with him made the retelling like new again.

Rachel was simply overwhelmed with everything she had learned this day, and she was too numb to say anything. She looked around to each one of the near strangers seated around her. This was her family. She was home. She allowed herself to lean back into the couch she shared with her twin brother, closed her eyes, and took in a deep breath.

Eleese reached over and took Rachel's hand in hers and gave it a gentle squeeze. Rachel opened her eyes and smiled at her mother. She seemed so composed considering the heartbreaking account she had just shared.

Therek and Lin got up to clear away the plates and food from lunch. Therek nodded toward Rachel saying, "Maybe when we return from the kitchen, we can give you a tour of the village for some much-needed fresh air and time to let this all sink in ... before we tell you the rest."

Rachel nodded in approval. Since both her grandparents were out of the room, Rachel looked to her mother and brother about her inner name. "I am wondering if it is something I've known all along, without knowing."

"Join hands with Rainor and relax your mind," Eleese suggested. "Try to look within and let the first thing that comes to your mind be spoken out loud." She turned to Rainor. "Hold the name inside,

but do not block it as you would do with others who may seek it for other reasons."

Rainor closed his eyes and did as his mother had requested. After a short time, Rachel felt very relaxed, though it was difficult to clear her mind. She tried to slow her breathing and think of nothing but the comfort her twin gave her. Slowly her thoughts melted away and she felt as if she and Rainor were the only two in the room.

[*Raiza, I'm elated to have found you. I know you are to be clearing your mind, but I need you to feel how complete I feel right now.*] Rainor's thoughts were like a comforting mental embrace around Rachel's swirling mind.

[*I feel the same, Therin.*] As if she had already been told, or knew it all along, not only did Rachel speak to Rainor's mind, she also used their shared inner name of *Therin*. The response Rachel made had caused both their eyes to shoot open.

Speaking to Rainor's mind was suddenly the easiest thing she had ever done. She couldn't explain it, but she could easily do it.

Tears of joy began to stream down Rachel's cheeks as she lunged forward to embrace Rainor. Eleese knew that the revelation of her inner name had been made. Upon their birth, they had shared their inner name with Eleese and Desmond. They concluded that the name must be a combination of Therek and Lin's names. It was fitting, to honor all they had done for Desmond and his mother. Eleese offered a slight smile and nod of recognition. When Therek and Lin rejoined them, Eleese shared the good news.

"You are now complete, my granddaughter," declared Therek as he offered her his arm for the tour, first of their home, then the village.

***

Therek and Lin's home was carved (or molded) into the very rocks that made up the cliffs. Some of the rooms' walls had been covered by a rattan covering, but others were left exposed. The glossy finish of the stone was smooth and dark with a texture that fascinated Rachel, like boiling lava had hardened with the rolling bubbles frozen in time.

Rachel couldn't help but gently run her fingers along the walls as they went from room to room.

Their home was simply decorated but breathtakingly beautiful. Petrified pieces of wood, rough rustic stone, or gemstones in various hues decorated the space. They rounded a corner at the far end of the lower floor, and Lin opened the door to one of their guest rooms. It would be Rachel's. Lin told her she was welcome to use it for as long as she desired. It was warm and inviting, with a view of the sea on the other side of the cliffs from the village.

Stones much like an opal were the focal point in the room, with a deep blue and silvery grey, stone tile floor, light aqua bedding and a sitting area to match. Between the high-backed chairs, there stood a low, rectangular, charcoal-colored, stone pillar the height of an end table. There was a clear basin resting on the top of the pillar.

Rachel walked over to examine it when Therek snapped his fingers. A soft blue fire ignited within the basin. Rachel gasped softly in amazement as she took another step closer.

"How did you …?" she mused as she snapped her own fingers, thinking the sound of it had somehow triggered the flames.

Therek laughed in amusement. "I have the ability to control fire and heat; I also used this power to mold the stone walls around you," he explained with a wave of his hand.

Rachel narrowed her eyes to examine the flame closer. "Do I need to invite you to my room to extinguish or reignite it?"

Again, he laughed. "No, dear. There is a lid to squelch it here and a flint to reignite it here," he said, motioning to the items mentioned.

Rainor shook his head and mumbled under his breath, "Show off."

"I heard that Rai," his grandfather clipped back with a grin.

Another young girl (more house help) brought down some fresh towels and soaps for Rachel to choose from. "Here are items for your bath. Will you need anything else to help you feel comfortable?"

Rachel couldn't think of anything else, "No, I don't think so. Thank you."

The girl glanced at Rachel's attire with a questioning look.

"Oh ... maybe some clothes to change into? I lost all of my gear," Rachel laughed nervously.

The girl smiled and gave a slight nod before leaving the room.

Rachel turned to Lin "Thank you so very much for the hospitality."

Lin chuckled, "You are with family now. No need to thank me."

They finished downstairs and went back to the main floor. From there, they showed her the meeting hall and told her they would be back there in the morning so the entire village could be properly introduced to her. In the meantime, this afternoon would be a short tour of the village, then back to their home to freshen up, eat, and get more acquainted.

The village was well organized and people were very friendly. She was introduced to only a few of the elves but word would spread quickly of her arrival. As they went along, Therek invited the elves to the meeting in the morning, and advised them to pass along the information to their neighbors. He wanted everyone in attendance.

Rachel was feeling nervous for the morning meeting. So many people would be there – all to see her.

As they walked, Eleese explained to Rachel more about why she and Rainor had been hidden. "Desmond and I were trying to figure out how we would convince the kingdom to accept our bond. In the meantime, we attempted to keep it a secret.

"Desmond's cousin, Stephan, was desperate to take the throne from Desmond. Stephan had sent spies to confirm the suspicions that Desmond had made forbidden contact with the elves. News of him having a child with one would surely put Stephan onto the throne. We knew our relationship could end Desmond's reign, but we could not deny our love.

"Eventually, Stephan had Desmond stripped of his crown and imprisoned. The other elves worried for the safety of you and your brother, so they devised a plan to hide you.

"There were two other mothers who had gone into labor within days of me. One family had lost their son, a very rare occurrence in our village and very sad. The other had a boy that was so similar in appearance to Rainor they could have been twins. The couple who lost their child allowed me to pretend he was mine. You can't imagine the heartache I felt for them. That little one was so beautiful, even in death. A tiny life lost," Eleese sighed deeply before continuing. "The other family – you'll meet them shortly – took Rainor in and pretended he was their own. Rainor mostly stayed with that other family, just for his safety.

"You were taken in by a human family and hidden all together until other arrangements could be made. If I had known what future lay ahead for you, I would never have agreed to this. At the time, it seemed the only way.

"The plan was to make it seem as if my child with Desmond had been lost. And it had worked. Word reached King Stephan that the child had died, and he did not send his soldiers to come searching for him, but Therek and Lin would not take any chances. They were not sure if Stephan was aware there had been two children born to us. We could not risk bringing you back to the village."

Rachel could sense the emotions of the ordeal even after all this time. She could see it on Eleese's face as if she was reliving it all over again. A flash of anger and hurt bubbled up inside of Rachel. Why did she have to be the one sent away? She forced those feelings back down. The past was behind her, there was no changing it. Despite Eleese's obvious turmoil, she remained regal and composed. Rachel wanted to emulate this quality. She marveled in the strength her mother possessed. She could forgive them, all of them. How could she not?

Rainor showed Rachel the home of his foster family as they approached. He went in without knocking and introduced her to his other family. The elves who took Rainor in looked more like him than Eleese did. Rachel searched her memory but couldn't remember what King Desmond had looked like. She was unaware how very much Rainor resembled their father.

The man, Rabb, and his wife, Tyne, were kind and seemed to be gentle, soft-spoken people. They welcomed Rachel and the others warmly and asked them to come in for a drink. It was a refreshing, minty drink with citrus undertones that cooled her throat as it went down. It quickly became Rachel's favorite.

Rainor raised a brow at her as she gulped down the first glass.

"I'm sorry, but that was delicious! I guess I didn't realize how thirsty I was ..." she said quietly. Her cheeks blushed, and she grinned apologetically. Tyne was more than happy to refill her glass. She tried to make this one last a bit longer.

"Rai and Sage are like brothers. We don't know what we would do without Rainor here to mellow our boy out," Rabb teased.

Rachel remembered meeting Sage as they entered the village; how could she forget?

They stayed for a short time to visit and Rachel watched the couple with interest. She could see the resemblance. She couldn't help but wonder though, *Were all the elves this attractive?* Rabb and Tyne were both tall, muscularly slender, with rich brown hair. It was obvious why the soldiers wouldn't have questioned Rainor as Rabb and Tyne's child. He looked just like them.

This family was so welcoming. Rachel enjoyed their company immensely. Tyne visited more with Eleese in the next room before they said their goodbyes. Rachel heard her refer to Rainor as her 'other son'.

Suddenly, Rachel's heart sank, and she felt overwhelmingly guilty. Her breathing sped up, her hands went to her face, and she whispered Jon's name. After all of the news she learned that day and the excitement of meeting her birth family and Rainor's foster family, she nearly forgot about her own foster family.

Rainor noticed her sudden discomfort and extended his arm to reach for her. He looked at his mother with a pleading glance. Eleese approached Rachel to see what had happened.

Rachel swallowed hard before quietly admonishing herself. "I almost forgot about Jon. How could I be so selfish?" her teary eyes filled with remorse.

Rabb got a chair for her and refilled her glass with water as they all attempted to convince her that everything was OK.

Eleese placed a healing hand on her shoulder to calm her. "Tell me, who is Jon? Why is this upsetting you so?"

"Jon is my foster brother. He is very ill, and I originally set out to find a healer for *him,* not to find my own family!" Rachel explained.

"Raiza, my sweet one, there is no reason for tears. You have not been selfish; do not beat yourself up over this. You have had quite a day!" Lin consoled her.

"Besides, you found what you were seeking, did you not?" Eleese added with all seriousness, "I will do my best to help you."

As Rachel looked to her mother, all her sadness and heartache melted away. Eleese had such a calming effect on her. She dried her tears and smiled at the group around her. They assured her they would all do what they could to help.

Just then, Sage burst through the door and spun around to slam it shut. As he fought to catch his breath, he motioned over his shoulder for the others to be quiet. Therek, Rabb, and Rainor immediately took a defensive stance. Tyne pulled Rachel back and Eleese and Lin moved to protect her. Instinctively, they readied for the worst, worrying that Rachel may have been followed.

A moment passed that felt like an eternity to Rachel as she wondered what sort of danger might burst in. She could sense the heightened awareness of her brother. Even though he seemed outwardly calm, he was anxious.

[*No one make a sound.*] Sage whispered through their minds without turning around. [*I'm going to look and see if I was followed.*] He moved slowly to the window.

Rachel's heartrate sped up. Sage's mental voice in her head felt foreign, different than Rainor's. Her mind flashed to the coyote-like creatures with too many teeth Rainor had told her about. *Could they be out there? Could it be soldiers of the king? Would they have been watching, waiting for my return?*

After peering out the window, Sage turned to the rest of the group. "OK, looks like I'm not being followed ..." he paused, took a look at everyone, and burst out laughing.

"What's wrong with you!" Rainor barked at him as they relaxed their stance.

Sage continued to laugh between phrases "The Flower Sisters ... oh you should have seen it! Boy, are they mad! They'll laugh about this later ... oh my sides ... then you guys! What's wrong with *me*? You all look like a war was to begin!" By this time he was bent over holding his gut.

Tyne threw her kitchen cloth at Sage. Therek and Rabb shook their heads at each other. Rainor was NOT amused. Now that his twin had returned and needed his help, he was a bit overprotective of her. His fists clenched every bit as much as his jaw, and Rachel grabbed his arm just before he raised it to swing at Sage. She got in front of him and offered a small smile (trying not to laugh now that the tension was broken) and hoped he would calm down.

"What?" Sage asked Rainor with his arms out and head cocked slightly to the side.

"I can't be around you right now. I thought you were in danger. I thought that *we* were in danger! We all thought that! An inconsiderate child is what you are ..." Rainor huffed as he pushed past Sage to exit the hut.

Sage turned to Therek and Rabb with an uncertain look of concern. Therek gently embraced Rachel's arm and brought her closer to face Sage. "I'm afraid Rainor's protective side has just found a reason to emerge," he spoke with a smile. "His sister has returned to us."

"His *sister*? It all makes sense now," Sage respectfully bowed to Rachel and took her hand to his cheek in a formal greeting.

Rachel blushed slightly at his tender touch.

Eleese excused herself to go outside and check on Rainor. He was pacing but had calmed down some. "I can't be mad at him for long. I'm not entirely sure what came over me, Mother," he admitted with a sigh.

"I know exactly what it was. Your sister was afraid." She held his face gently in her hands as he looked down at her. "With your skills of communication and hers of healing, even untapped as they are, the longer you two are together, the more connected you will become."

Rainor took a deep breath, hugged his mother, and they went back inside.

Sage spun around on his heels and extended an arm to apologize. Rainor playfully slapped it away and made his own apology for overreacting. "Since she's your sister, and not your secret lover, may I join you for the remainder of your outing?" Sage cracked a mischievous smile at Rachel, making her blush again. At this, the small group laughed and left to finish the village tour. As they went along, Therek continued to invite others to the morning meeting in the great hall and asked that they spread the word.

Eleese and Lin asked Rachel more about Jon's condition as they walked. "What symptoms does he display?" Lin questioned.

"How long has he been ill?" Eleese added.

They were gathering information to better understand how to heal the boy. They decided to take Rachel back to her room when they had to wait for information between tired pauses and yawns. She truly had been through quite a day. Upon arrival back at Therek and Lin's home, Rainor, Sage and Eleese excused themselves to their own homes while Rachel was taken to her room to rest and freshen up.

"You have no need to rush, dear," Lin assured her. "Relax and indulge in the warmth of a bath. We will not dine until sunset."

By Rachel's guess, she had about two glorious hours of relaxing to do. She would relish every minute of it. The young girl from earlier had left a soap for Rachel that smelled of honeysuckle. The stone tub was large and deep enough to sink down all the way beneath the water. The soap felt like pure silk on her skin, she had never felt anything like it. Rachel submerged in the warmth of the water and felt her tired body relax. She came up to rest her head at the edge of the tub and closed her eyes. After the heat of the water began to fade, she emerged feeling completely clean and pampered. She wrapped herself in a towel, braided her hair, and went to the bed chamber.

A fresh set of clothes had been placed neatly at the foot of the bed; there lay a flowing cream-colored tunic and wine-colored leggings with soft slippers. She gladly put them on. After days of travel, the clean clothes felt wonderful. She walked to the large window to gaze at the sea. It was so peaceful. She must have remained there for half an hour.

There was a quiet knock at the door. She smiled up at Rainor as she opened it. He offered his arm and asked if she was ready to join them up in the dining room. She reached up and allowed him to escort her.

"Do you mind that Sage, Rabb, and Tyne will be joining us?"

"Of course not! I am already very fond of your 'other family'." She gave his arm a little squeeze.

Once they rounded the top of the stairs, Rachel could hear the others visiting, and she could smell a savory aroma that made her mouth water. She closed her eyes and inhaled deeply through her nose. As she exhaled, she made an 'mmm' sound she hadn't intended to be audible.

Rainor laughed. "Lamb stew tonight."

There was an enormous amount of food set neatly on the table. Every bit of it needed tasting. Rachel hadn't had a meal like this in years. In addition to the stew, there were soft warm rolls, a variety of freshly cut fruits and vegetables, and a heated bowl of sweet bread with braised apples and cold sweetened cream to top it with.

After everyone was seated and began dishing up their food, conversations continued. The others had many questions for Rachel. She didn't mind being the one to do most of the talking in this wonderful group. They made her completely at ease. She told them of her childhood and her foster family, but mostly of Jon. Eleese assured her that with Rachel's help, she could heal him – if the Mills would accept her help.

Rachel wasn't sure what Jack and Mavis would do when they saw her with a band of elves at her side. She was even more unsure of Eleese's faith in her ability to help with Jon's healing.

"Tomorrow after the village meeting, we will make plans to get you back to Jon. Therek and I will delegate others to join us, and we will leave the following morning," Eleese told her. "I also want to work with you some on your talents. I have already sensed that you have great strength, but you lack the knowledge of how to use it. You mentioned before that Jon seemed to feel more comfortable with you, did you not?" she questioned Rachel with one brow raised, not waiting for a reply. "That is because your basic nature was already attempting to reach out to him. I am very optimistic. We will travel a different route than how you arrived, and it will take less time."

Lin patted Rachel's hand and said she would join them for Rachel's training. Everyone else joined in together with positive thoughts and encouraging words so it sounded like an encouraging buzz from all around her.

Rachel only had one request. "Will you please allow your people to volunteer for this trip, rather than to delegate them? I would hate for anyone to feel obligated to do this, just because of who I am to you."

Rainor smiled at Therek and Eleese, knowing the reason for the delegation would not be to get enough help, but rather to thin the crowd. After all, they knew the whole village might try to step up.

During the meal, Rachel had remembered Rainor mentioning their destiny and that their meeting was nearly two years past due. She decided that she needed to know what the future held for her, and now was as good a time as any to ask. "Rainor, earlier you mentioned that we were to have met much earlier, to 'fulfill our destiny'. What exactly *was* the plan?"

Rainor wasn't sure how to begin as he knew this topic would only add to Rachel's feelings of being overwhelmed. Her relentless stare bore into him. He felt compelled to tell her, but paused, unsure how to begin.

Eleese gave him a look to excuse him from explaining it as she replied for him. "Your life will soon be changed. You will not only learn more about your healing gifts, but you will also need to learn the ways of battle. Legend tells that you and your brother were born to lead this land and bring balance back to its inhabitants. Humans, though we're not certain how many, and elves alike are depending on this legend to free us of the tyrant we now call king.

"I know this is all a lot to take in, but if King Stephan is allowed to marry and if an heir is born before your twenty-first birthday, you will lose your rights to the throne. I am afraid that poverty and desperation will rule this land under his continued reign. From the sound of things, he has already chosen a bride. Though arrangements may not be solidified yet, we haven't much time to make our move. You will need to muster all the courage you have."

Eleese was correct – it was an extremely daunting realization for Rachel. Being overwhelmed was the theme for the day it seemed. As with the rest of the information she had been given, she allowed this to sink in and gradually accepted it. There was no more floating through life for Rachel.

After the meal was finished and everyone was full to their capacity, not only of food but of information as well, Rabb, Sage, Therek, and Rainor helped the kitchen staff clear the table. The staff then went about cleaning up after the meal.

The two families returned to the sitting room to relax and further discuss the following days. Eleese left the room for a brief time with Lin then returned with two small boxes. They were no bigger than Eleese's hand, black, and very ornately carved. Rachel couldn't help feeling curious as to the contents. Lin and Eleese sat on either side of Rachel and Rainor as Eleese cleared her throat to get everyone's attention. When the room was quiet, Eleese presented one of the boxes to Rachel as she bowed her head slightly.

"I have waited many years to present this to you. Please ... open it."

Rachel traced her finger over the top of the box. As she did, the solid black color started to change and shapes began to appear. It was decorated with a heart that had three ribbons entwined around it. One delicate, silver ribbon, one thin, deep red ribbon, and one bold, copper ribbon stood out against the black. The copper ribbon wound its way around the entire box. Her hands began to tingle as she opened the lid. She wasn't sure if it was from the anticipation or if there was some magic at work. She could see that Eleese was very interested in her reaction. Rachel gazed, mouth agape, at the intricate, copper bracelet inside. It was very much like the redone Eleese wore. Rachel then noticed Therek and Lin's bracelets as well.

When Rachel took her bracelet from the box, it glimmered and seemed to hum. She thought maybe she was imagining it until Rainor whispered to her, "Is it humming?"

The room had been totally silent until she had touched the bracelet, and everyone agreed they had heard the humming as well.

Lin spoke up. "These are no ordinary bracelets," she said pointing to her own, Therek's, and Eleese's. "The box reveals a person's talents or gifts by the image and the color of the ribbons. The most prominent ribbon magically changes the color of the bracelet itself to match. Each color holds a different meaning; copper is something unseen for many generations. The silver ribbon represents a gentle soul, the red stands for honor or loyalty, and the copper speaks to Rachel's future as a great leader."

"There is more to your destiny than we can even imagine," Therek exclaimed. "You will do great things, little one."

Rachel couldn't help but blush and didn't know what to say. She slid the bracelet over her left hand and it settled against her skin. It was so light weight and warmed instantly, making it extremely comforting to wear.

Eleese then told her the heart in the middle confirmed she would be a very talented healer. Rachel thanked Eleese with a tight hug. It was Rainor's turn to receive his. As Eleese handed him the box, he almost dropped it, experiencing the same tingling sensation that Rachel had.

He glanced over at her with wide eyes as she stifled a giggle. "Tingles huh?" she asked, already knowing the answer.

Rainor's box revealed an eye along with three ribbons: one of blue, the same red as Rachel's, and the third the same bold copper as well. Everyone gasped in awe – two copper ribbons. Therek couldn't help but stand a little taller for the pride he felt. The

eye on Rainor's box symbolized his honesty and
ability to see others' truths. The blue ribbon stood
for great courage.

Rainor decided to wear his on the right arm,
smiling at the gift as he admired it. Where Rachel's
bracelet was petite and thin with minute swirling
patterns, Rainor's was twice as thick and etched with
a chevron pattern. They both gleamed in the light.

"I couldn't be more proud," Therek
whispered to Rabb, "though I'm not all that surprised
at the outcomes." He tapped his own blue bracelet.
At this, they all laughed.

The bracelets were made for the family of the
chief by an elderly elf, the mother of Therek's
advisor. She had been the advisor for Therek's father
and possessed many magical powers. Of those, she
passed on the power of future sight to her son,
Jarrell. Jarrell's daughter, Kaiya, was also blessed
with the powers of her grandmother and would
someday take her father's place, becoming an
advisor for Eleese.

While Rachel and Rainor sat admiring their
bracelets, Eleese told them more of the route they
would take to Rachel's foster parents. "I have an old
friend between Geerda and Brimley that we can visit
on the way. Her home is south of where Rachel had

traveled, and that route should cut a few days off the travel time."

By this time, Rachel was desperately trying to keep her eyes open. After her long, relaxing bath and a full belly, her exhaustion was winning out. Rabb, Tyne and Sage said their goodnights and Therek took Rainor aside to discuss something with him before he too said goodnight.

Eleese and Lin took Rachel to her room. Once they had a few more moments to talk, and Rachel got settled in, Lin hugged her once more, "I will see you in the morning".

Eleese placed her thin hand to Rachel's cheek briefly then she and Lin excused themselves back upstairs.

"I can't believe this moment is finally here," Eleese whispered to her mother.

"I feel a sense of great fulfillment. Good night; I will see *you* in the morning too."

Merri Gammage

TRAVEL DAY NINE

"Welcome all! Please settle," Therek proclaimed as the meeting was about to begin.

Nearly all of the villagers were present, which made the meeting hall quite crowded. Everyone was anxious to meet Raiza. They had heard the rapidly spread rumors of her return but not the details of how or why she had arrived now – nearly two years after they had expected her. Therek, Lin, Eleese, Rainor, and Rachel stood at the front of the room. All but Rachel were regal and beaming with pride. Rachel chewed her bottom lip and fiddled with the end of her braid, nervous and anxious. Rainor gave her a reassuring smile as Therek officially called the meeting to order.

"Friends, we have called this meeting to share some wonderful news with all of you. For many years, we have been waiting for this time – the time for the prophecy of old to come to light. For many years, we have worried this time would not be. After losing contact with our human friends, Brock and Rebecca, who were kind enough to take on the task of raising our little Raiza, we feared the worst. However, the circumstances may be different than we planned for, but fate has brought Raiza home at last!" With this statement, Therek raised his arm to motion her over to his side. The whole room erupted in cheers and applause.

Rachel was overjoyed by their enthusiasm. Therek and Rachel gave a brief history, as much as they knew, of how she came about returning, and then allowed for questions. When the time came to tell of their journey to heal Jon, Rachel was amazed at how many volunteers stepped forth to join her. Now she understood the reason for delegation.

Rainor elbowed her and said, "See? I knew they'd all be eager to help out. Only the most young and most elderly are not volunteering for the trip."

"I would like those of you with children to stay behind. There will be some dangers to be faced," Eleese announced. That helped to thin the crowd down to about a third of the village left hoping to be selected. "We will only be selecting a small travel party. We don't wish to draw too much attention as we go."

"Lin and I will remain here, and I feel that most of our guards should stay as well ... though at least one could be spared," Therek added.

After much discussion and crowd-thinning while Rachel visited with everyone, the decision was made. Eleese, Rainor, and Rachel would be joined by Sage, Aryn, Rik, and Lea.

Rachel was already comfortable with Sage and appreciated his humor. He was quite good with a sword. Aryn was one of the tree guards and excellent with a bow. Rachel found him to be overly serious and unapproachable. Rik was one of the village's strongest fighters and possibly knew every plant that existed. He appeared older than the rest. Lea was instantly Rachel's favorite. She was beautifully tall and moved with such grace. She was a fine swordsman and skilled huntress and tracker, but it was her easy-going personality that Rachel was drawn to.

Congratulations were given by the other villagers as they left to go about their day. Dinner was brought in for the selected group. They sat and discussed the arrangements for their trip. It was obvious to Rachel that some of this group was already friendly toward each other, while others were no more than acquaintances.

She studied each one, not only their personalities but physical appearances as well. Rainor and Sage were so handsome with their deep brown hair and tall, muscular physiques. Rik was shorter and had a broader stature, twice the muscles of the younger men, but no less handsome. He had shoulder length, salt and pepper hair and a neatly-trimmed beard. He carried himself with maturity and confidence. Lea was striking to look at. She was an inch taller than Rainor and had dark brown, almost black hair that flowed freely down her back. She was graceful in her movements and had tanned skin and dark eyes. Rachel had never seen anyone quite like her. She appeared to be most comfortable with Sage and Rainor. *Was she completely unaware of her beauty?* She and Rachel immediately hit it off.

Then there was Aryn. He barely spoke a word and seemed so set on only discussing the journey and nothing else in detail. He was not unkind, but there was something about him that seemed mysterious and secretive to Rachel. She trusted Therek and Eleese's decision on their group, but he cast some minor doubts in her mind. She wasn't sure how he would fit in as the rest of the group was already opening up to each other and seemed very relaxed.

Rachel decided to keep an eye on Aryn. He was another very good-looking elf, so she decided she really didn't mind the task she had set for herself. Aryn was two inches, maybe three, taller than Rainor, had short blond hair, just long enough in front to partially hide one of his hazel eyes. He was tanned bronze from being in the tree-tops so much and had a lean, muscular build; it was perfect … for climbing trees.

Does he ever smile?

"Rachel … Rachel? Hey!" Rainor finally got her attention.

"Oh! Sorry, I was just … um … thinking of our journey," she stammered with a touch of embarrassment. "How is it that everyone in this village is so attractive?" she whispered.

Rainor looked at her with confusion and shrugged his shoulders. "I guess I never noticed it before." His eyes scanned the group, pausing for a moment longer on Lea.

"Well, you'll see what I mean when you are around full-on humans in the area I grew up. Maybe it is because everyone has to work so hard, I don't know ..." she trailed off, looking down at nothing in particular.

"Well, now I've forgotten what I was going to say ..." Rainor had to admit.

Rachel was soon conversing with Lea and Rik when Eleese took her leave. She had asked Rainor to tell Rachel to join her after the others departed. She was on the beach waiting for Rachel. She sat tall with her legs crossed and her eyes closed, enjoying the sounds of the sea as it caressed the pebbly sand.

Rachel was excited to begin her training with her mother. It still felt so surreal ... *my mother*. She excused herself from the table, walked to the beach, quietly approached and sat next to Eleese. She studied Eleese's features, so like her own.

"I want you to understand where your powers come from," began Eleese without changing her position. "So, the first test I shall give you should help identify that. Please do not be angered by what I am about do," and without even looking, she snatched up a small crab scuttling by and broke off one of its claws. She then handed the crab to Rachel.

At first Rachel was upset and, indeed, almost angry. She hated to see an innocent animal suffer. As she held the crab in her hands, she could feel a place in her heart stir like she had never felt before.

"Now, I assume you have already begun to feel your powers churning inside of you. Focus that feeling on wanting to help that crab's injury," Eleese advised.

Rachel closed her eyes to help her focus and within a few minutes heard herself yelp. She felt a firm pinch to the skin between her thumb and index finger. She accidentally dropped the little crab.

Her mother stifled a laugh. "Look at the crab, Raiza," she advised.

The crab was whole again and had pinched her with the very claw she had regrown for it! She looked at Eleese, eyes wide in utter wonderment.

"Your first try, I *knew* you were especially gifted," Eleese complimented her daughter.

"You're not going to hurt any more animals though, are you?" Rachel asked with a frown.

Eleese assured her there was no need. "We have an infirmary that has a few injured or sick right now. Lin will meet us there. I usually go there about this time of day to oversee our other healer. You'll like him. He's younger than you and still in training, but I trust him to run things while we are away. Let's go and see what assistance we can offer."

Rachel felt a bit timid but went along. "I won't hurt anyone if I do something wrong, will I?" she asked as she fiddled with her hair.

"No, nothing I can't help you to correct. Unless you harbor anger toward someone, only comfort and healing can occur. Try not to touch people when you are terribly angry with them though, until you are fully trained at least. You can cause serious injury out of anger."

Rachel nodded her understanding.

When they arrived at the infirmary, Lin was speaking to a young boy with sandy brown hair. "Mother, Elman, hello," Eleese greeted them, "Elman, this is my daughter, Raiza."

Elman was almost the same height as Rachel and had a kind face. He extended his arm to greet her. "Hello, and welcome home. Maybe you both can assist me with something." He was eager to get some help with one of the injured guards-in-training who had just torn open his hand quite badly on a branch that had been splintered by lightning in the recent storm. "He's pretty bad, and I'm not sure I'm up for the challenge."

He could heal an illness far better than a wound. When they came around to the bed, Elman led them to, another young boy sat holding his right hand in a bloody cloth. He smiled sheepishly at Rachel. It was the same boy she had waved at when she arrived the day before. It suddenly dawned on her that Aryn had been the one who elbowed him. He must have been the one doing the training.

"This is my friend, Sym. He's training to be a guard!" Elman announced proudly. He admired his friend a great deal. Rachel wondered how old these boys were; they seemed awfully young.

"Hello, Sym. I believe I saw you in the trees yesterday, if I'm not mistaken?" Rachel asked.

Being seen as a guard was unacceptable. He had been reprimanded for it by Aryn and felt ashamed. His smile faded, his gaze fell to the floor.

"I'm sorry," Rachel carefully placed his injured hand in hers, sensing his shame. "I was *thrilled* to see you guys up there! Especially after Rainor had told me we had been watched for so long. I never would have known you were all up there if he hadn't told me."

Sym raised his head and smiled. He was a cutie with dark hair, freckles, and large, dark brown eyes. Rachel asked if she could look at his hand and he agreed, removing the bandage carefully. Lin was unsure that Rachel was up to the task, but Eleese put a hand on Sym's shoulder and verbally walked Rachel through what to focus on first. Because his hand would be so important to his guard duties and using a bow, they needed to make sure every nerve and muscle fiber was back in place.

Once again, Rachel closed her eyes to focus. She was nervous. Eleese helped her. "Breathe evenly. Visualize every part of the hand."

Rachel had never before thought how intricate the *inside* of someone could be! The gift she was born with began to take over, and she could feel the magical properties guiding her moves. Beyond the skin, muscle fibers and tendons became visible in her mind's eye. It was an incredible feeling to be able to see every part of his internal workings.

Eleese's inner voice guided Rachel through each step. [*Focus on the bones. They appear intact. Next, check each fiber as it connects to the bone ... not so fast ... make it match the other hand. See how it should be... careful now...*] Through her touch, she could see what Rachel was seeing, and calmly redirected Rachel when she needed it. [*Now, focus on each place he is losing blood. One by one, mend the tears. Next, move on to the muscle ... that's it... you're doing well.*]

Rachel had to remind herself to breathe but otherwise, she was feeling quite proud of her accomplishments until one muscle section frustrated her. Sym winced in pain as Rachel lost sight of her task and incorrectly attached the muscle to the wrong location. Rachel could see that it was not right, but wasn't sure what to do.

Lin stepped forward but Eleese motioned to her that it would be alright. Eleese took the hand to administer some pain relief and disconnect what Rachel had done. Rachel was very apologetic as she began the task again, this time not allowing herself a victory celebration until she was completely done.

The healing took nearly thirty minutes and Rachel felt drained afterwards, but Sym clapped his hands and wiggled all his fingers as he told her it was as good as new.

Eleese was very proud of her daughter. She was in awe at how very skilled she was, considering her lack of training. Rachel was a naturally gifted healer. Lin got a cool drink and some cheese for Rachel.

"That was incredible!" Rachel felt certain she could not have done that all by herself. "Thank you for the guidance and the opportunity," she mumbled around the bite she was chewing.

"You have surpassed my expectations, especially so soon after your first attempt!" Eleese was truly amazed.

Elman just stood there with his mouth half open. Eleese gave him a reassuring pat. "Your powers will get stronger with age."

"If I may ask, how old are you, Elman?" inquired Rachel.

"Sym and I are both fourteen. We have the same birthday! But we're not twins or anything like you and Rainor, just friends – the best of friends." Both boys smiled broadly.

Lin confessed, "I may have been overly concerned during the process. I'm sorry that I doubted you both."

"I was even less confident in my abilities than either of you!" Rachel told her grandmother, and they laughed together at the relief they felt after the whole experience.

Eleese dismissed Sym and left Elman with instructions to follow while she was away. She assured him that Lin would be glad to assist if he needed her.

Rachel was impressed with the responsibility those boys had at such a young age. They already knew their life path, something Rachel wasn't even sure of at nineteen. Eleese and Rachel excused themselves to move on.

"I began helping out here when I was almost sixteen, but Elman is already showing more skill than I possessed at that age. He will be a great healer as he grows," Eleese confessed.

They made their way through the infirmary, stopping on occasion to help, and were about to leave when Rachel noticed a very small girl under one of the beds. She bent down to see why she was under the bed and not on it. The little girl grinned at her and thrust out her tiny hand, carefully wrapped around something she must have felt was precious.

"Hello there, what have you got?" asked Rachel.

"Theeds," lisped the tiny child and opened her hand to show Rachel. "I foun 'em by my thlipper!" she said with excitement. "Watch THITH!" She spit into her hand.

Rachel pulled her head back wondering what the child could possibly be doing, then her eyes grew wide. There, in the child's palm, a tiny plant began to grow.

Eleese gently picked the child up and put her on the bed. "Very good, Timly! You are obviously feeling a bit better, yes?"

"Yeth, Eleethe, Elman thayz I can go home thoon," she cooed at the little sprout as she spoke.

"Good to hear that. When I come back from my travels, I will bring you some new seeds to grow!" Eleese patted the girl's head and brought Rachel outside after they said goodbye to Timly, and Elman, who was just coming to check on his favorite little patient. "Timly is one of the most gifted tree benders our village has ever seen. She is only four years old and already manipulating small seeds and plants. One day she will be a guardian of our forest. She strained herself trying to fix a full-grown tree a few days ago, but she's learning her limits. You will soon learn yours as well, I believe you will excel in injury healing, but we have yet to see how you will fare with an illness. They are different indeed."

She explained further as they made their way to the meeting hall. "When you are healing an injury, there is great focus needed to see how the damaged body part *should* have been, so you can put it back together the way it was prior to the injury. Think of it like a picture puzzle game. The whole creates an intricate picture but when the picture is broken apart, it may be difficult to determine what it should look like. It makes it somewhat easier to look to the other side of the body if you are repairing parts with a symmetrical counterpart, like I had you do with Sym's hand.

"An illness is a whole different matter. Most of us excel in either one or the other. You have shown great skill in injury healing. When we assess Jon, we will not be repairing a broken picture but rather trying to clean it up. Imagine if the picture puzzle game was complete, with all of its pieces intact, but someone had spilled something across it, making the picture blurred and discolored. When you heal an illness, it is like trying to clean off the stains while leaving the picture underneath unharmed. It can be tremendously straining on both the healer and the patient. I usually try to begin an illness healing with warmth and feelings of peace or joy. Often times, the patient's body will react positively and try to help out with the process. It is difficult to say how things will go with Jon though.

Once I can meet with him, I should have a better idea of how to help," Eleese gave Rachel a confident smile.

Eleese and Rachel met up with Rainor, Sage, Aryn, Rik, and Lea. They had been preparing and nearly gathered all the supplies the group would need for the following days' journey and decided it was as good a time as any to take a break. They reported their progress to Eleese.

"Well then, it sounds to me that you all deserve a little free time before we finalize everything. Let's plan to meet back in the meeting hall for dinner at sunset. Then we can finish packing any last items and get a good night's rest. We will leave quite early." Eleese was proud of the hard-working individuals they had selected.

The group decided to go to the beach to relax with a couple games using various colored tiles or rocks. They agreed it would be good for Rachel to learn since all the villagers knew the games well, and they didn't want her to feel left out if she ever came back for a visit. The afternoon sun was warm and a slight breeze brought the smell of the sea across the sand.

Aryn decided to excuse himself to meet up with some of the other guards and check on Sym.

When Rachel told him she had healed his hand and that he was no longer in the infirmary, he just nodded and left.

She turned to Lea and rolled her eyes. "He's sort of a stick-in-the-mud, isn't he?" she whispered with a laugh. Lea laughed as well as they linked arms to stroll along the beach.

Rik decided to go in the water as he had done much of the heavy loading of the food wagon they were to take along. He undressed down to his undergarments with not a care and walked into the surf. Rachel and Lea exchanged a comical glance and broke out into laughter yet again.

Rainor and Sage set up the gameboard on a large, flat rock and Lea explained the rules to Rachel. The first game was fast paced and simple. Each player had three tiles of their color and moved them around the board by the roll of the dice. If one person's tile was in a spot and your tile landed upon the same spot, you could capture their tile. Whoever captured the most tiles was the winner. After a couple rounds, Sage was losing horribly and decided to get in the water instead. Rik came over to take his place. After a short time, Rik excused himself to spend some time with his bond-mate; he would miss her greatly while he was away. Everyone else stayed to play.

On more than one occasion, Rachel felt they were being watched. She silently communicated this to Rainor. [*I think someone is watching us.*]

[*There shouldn't be any dangers at this section of the beach, besides...*] He paused to make a move in the game before continuing. [*If there was, the guards would have sent us all a silent warning.*]

She still felt something though. Rainor's inner voice seemed different than it had before too. It made her uncomfortable and distracted which made her lose at the second game they played (a strategy game), so she rotated out.

She began to scan the nearby trees for any sign of something or someone. Then she figured it out. It was Aryn. She didn't want him to know she had spotted him, so she acted as if she hadn't, and shrugged it off. She jogged down to the water's edge and walked along, allowing the edges of the lapping waves to tickle her toes as she looked at pebbles and shells.

[*Rainor, it's Aryn ... don't look ... but he's watching us from the fourth tree in from the giant rock.*]

[*So he is. Is he upsetting you?*] Rainor didn't want Rachel to be uncomfortable. He knew Aryn's family well, but Aryn had always been a bit quiet and hard to get to know. He was well respected, but Rainor wasn't sure if he had many real friends. He was only a few years older than Rainor and Sage but always acted much more serious and mature – a real 'duty first' kind of guy.

[*No, he is not upsetting me, but I feel like I need to figure him out...*]

[*OK, if you would rather, I can ask mother to select someone else?*]

[*NO... no no... that isn't at all necessary. I mean, he's already packed and ready to go... it will be fine.*]

Rainor laughed out loud, Rachel glared at him, and the others looked between them oddly, but he waved it off. They seemed content not to inquire further.

Eventually, everyone ended up in the water, throwing seaweed at each other and getting sand everywhere. They had great fun, and Rachel was very much at ease and looking forward to her journey home with her new friends and her brother.

Nearly four hours had passed since they got to the beach and the evening air took on a chill. The friends dried themselves off, packed up the games, and made their way back to the village to clean up before supper.

Aryn was still in the same tree Rachel had seen him in earlier, and she couldn't help but let Lea in on the secret. She didn't seem surprised. As they passed nearby, Rachel said, "Too bad Aryn couldn't have joined us. He missed all the fun..." She turned just in time to lock eyes with him and to catch what appeared to be a hint of a smile tugging at one corner of his mouth. He quickly regained his composure and ducked back behind the other trees. The two girls giggled as they ran to catch up with the others.

After everyone had gotten cleaned up, they met for supper in the meeting hall. Aryn was there first and Rachel second. "I hope you're not too terribly mad that I saw you in the trees by the beach," she said softly as she approached him. He was standing in front of one of the large windows that looked out to the sea. He slowly turned just his head toward her and gave her a smirk.

Rik and Sage came in laughing about something and broke the short, but palpable, tension.

Shortly after that, Eleese and Lea arrived with Rainor close behind.

The house help was bringing out trays of food and getting the table set. Everyone began to take their seats. There was a salad served with several garden vegetables, a savory broth, and a roast that had been rolled with a bread stuffing in the middle. The group discussed their plans for the following few days and Eleese produced a map to show everyone the route. Rachel was happy they would pass through the same path in the forest; she was hoping to run into the bushkins again.

The meal ended and dessert was brought out. A large bowl with various berries was placed in the center of the table with a smaller bowl filled with sweetened cream. It reminded Rachel of the little cottage where she had learned of the way into the forest. She found where the cottage was on the map. "Will we able to stop here, so I can at least thank the little family that helped me find my way into the forest?"

"It is not on our route, but we have much respect for Forrin and his family. I will send a rider to request that he meet us at the Twin Tree," Eleese replied.

"Thank you so very much!" Rachel was pleased and thankful for the consideration.

The group agreed to meet back at the meeting hall two hours before dawn. As darkness set in and they all retired to their own homes or rooms, Rachel's head swam as she wondered how would she get *any* sleep tonight.

TRAVEL DAY TEN

A young girl, one of the house helpers, came into Rachel's room to wake her, but she was already awake. Her sleep had not been as sound as she would have liked. She was anxious to get on the road.

It took very little time for Rachel to get ready. She changed back into her travel clothes; they had been cleaned for her. There were two other outfits given to her. She grabbed those up and put the box her bracelet had come in into a bag. She brought everything up to the meeting hall.

Aryn stood by the door cleaning his dagger and glanced up but said nothing.

"Good morning to you too," Rachel teased.

"I'm afraid I'm not as rested as I should be," he replied, returning his gaze to the well-polished blade.

"Well, that makes two of us, I suppose," she said with a yawn. "I had too much on my mind last night."

"I imagine so," was all he said in response.

Rachel stood staring at him for a moment, admiring his features in the dim torchlight outside the meeting hall. *Will he be like this the whole journey? Or will he eventually open up?*

[*Deep thoughts for this early in the morning. I still need to teach you to separate your private thoughts from your general mind sharing,*] Rainor sent his words to her mind.

Her eyes grew larger and she turned to her twin as he approached. She was afraid that if he could 'hear' her thoughts, Aryn could also. She tried to clear her mind, which only seemed to make it more difficult to stop thinking of things.

Rainor greeted Aryn and asked if he minded if he and Rachel stepped into Therek and Lin's home for a brief moment. Aryn nodded casually so they stepped aside and went in. Rainor led Rachel into one of the empty guest rooms. "I don't think Aryn heard or sensed your thoughts, but your control is in need of some work."

Rachel sighed in relief, "Oh thank goodness. That surely would have made this journey uncomfortable!"

"These rooms are enchanted, so your thoughts are your own, unless you will them to be shared. I think that because we are so near to these rooms, your thoughts may have been partially protected, but maybe because of the close bond we share, we may be a little more sensitive toward each other's thoughts. I could *hear* what you were thinking. But like I said, I don't think Aryn could," Rainor explained. "I want you to close your eyes and mind-speak something to me that is not private; focus on those words and how you are projecting them," he instructed her.

[*Who do you suppose will show up last?*] she asked Rainor.

"Now, when you spoke that to me, it took more focus, because of where we are. Did you notice anything about those words as you thought them?" he questioned.

"They seemed to be written boldly in my mind," Rachel said in awe.

"That's because they were willed to be shared. Everyone close by probably 'heard' them but they know you were most likely directing them to me since you haven't shared your thoughts intentionally with anyone else yet. Now try to focus even more and direct something else right to me … and only me," he coaxed.

[*I bet it will be Sage.*]

This time as she thought the words carefully to her brother, they appeared much lighter in her mind, not as heavily scripted in her imagination. She looked up at him and asked if it had worked.

[*Yes, it did, and I agree with you,*] he laughed back in her thoughts. "Now, when you don't want anyone else to hear your thoughts, they should be directed internally and may show with no significance or not at all in your mind's eye."

She could now see that not only were her thoughts to him less bold, but his incoming thoughts were as well. "So that's how I can tell if you are directing your thoughts privately, or to everyone?"

"You've got it. It isn't difficult. You just need to focus, and with time, it will be like second nature," he said with a grin. As he began to leave the room, he privately shared one more thought. [*Yesterday on the beach, he could hear your thoughts when you noticed him in the trees.*] Then, with a mischievous grin, he bolted out the door to meet up with everyone else. Rachel felt her face flush with embarrassment.

Rachel mustered up the courage to rejoin Rainor and Aryn outside. She was pleased to see that Therek and Lin were just behind her to bid farewell to the group. Just before the three exited the home, Lin gently grabbed Rachel's hand and smiled a sad smile at her.

[*I already miss you; promise me you will return one day,*] Lin's loving message warmed Rachel's mind.

[*Of course I will!*] Rachel sent back to her grandmother as she turned to embrace her. Now that she knew the difference between how to send her thoughts, it gave a thrill that interrupted her emotions, if only for a moment.

Therek remained silent but lovingly placed a hand on each of their shoulders as they made their way outside. Rachel tried to avoid looking in Aryn's direction.

Rainor's smirk faded as he realized the gravity of the situation facing Rachel. She had never known this family and now, after only a short time with them, was having to say goodbye to her grandparents. He could feel her emotions surfacing.

Rik, Lea, Eleese, and Sage arrived shortly thereafter, snapping Rachel into more focus. The group made sure everything was in order for their journey.

"I have sent Breeze ahead to send your message to Forrin," Eleese told Rachel. "She should be there before midday as she left yesterday evening and is on our fastest horse."

"Thank you, Mother, for everything," Rachel choked out as a tear slid down her cheek. She was feeling a myriad of emotions; it was all very overwhelming.

"We had better get going," Aryn cut in coolly as he mounted his horse. Rachel briefly glared at the back of his head as he turned, trying to keep her thoughts to herself. *Couldn't he at least try to show some compassion?*

Rachel closed her eyes and took in a deep, calming breath; she had to remember that they were all going on this journey together ... for her.

The group finished saying goodbye and departed the village quickly in the dark of early morning. Eleese took the lead with Rik and Lea directly behind her, Rachel and Rainor to follow, and Aryn and Sage in the back. The food wagon was fixed to Sage's horse for now, but would be easily undone to rotate around between them as they traveled. No one spoke a word aloud.

After some time with nothing to break the silence, Rachel began to feel uneasy. The cool morning caused her to shiver and she glanced at Rainor, wondering if she should say something.

[*The forest can be a dangerous place this early,*] Rainor thought to Rachel, already able to sense her concerns. [*After the sun comes up, the journey will become more pleasant,*] he assured her with a nod.

The horses continued on at a trot. The crunching of their hooves on the gravel road was the only sound Rachel could hear. [***So … how did everyone else sleep last night?***] Rachel sent out to her travel companions, trying to fight off boredom and drowsiness. Each one responded in a brief manner that suggested their attention was elsewhere. Rachel didn't bother asking anything further.

[*Don't take it personally; they don't want to frighten you. We are sensing something following us. Don't panic! It is probably nothing of danger, but they are trying to protect you,*] Rainor explained privately to Rachel.

As they continued on, Rachel could sense the tension in the rest of the group and began to focus on calming thoughts for the rest of her companions, hoping it would work.

[*That will be enough of that,*] an unfamiliar inner voice cut through Rachel's mind causing her eyes to snap open. She had a feeling it was Aryn, but did not want to reply or turn to make eye contact. She was still frustrated with him. One awkward moment with him was enough.

"You OK?" Rainor mouthed to her, barely audible. She smiled and nodded even though she still felt uneasy about their ride so far.

Eleese suddenly brought them to a halt, silently giving instructions to the others. Rik turned his horse around to guard Rachel from the left, Lea moved the rump of her horse in front of Rachel with the head in front of Rainor. Aryn moved to Rainor's right, facing Lea. Sage easily disconnected the food wagon from his horse with two quick clicks and moved to his position at the back, facing Rik.

Rachel's heart began to pound in her chest; obviously there was something going on that they weren't telling her. [*Rainor!*] She pleaded with her brother.

Eleese slowly circled the group, scanning the still dark forest around them. A noise, so terrifying that it made Rachel jump, sounded from behind them toward the right. It was a high-pitched howl that seemed to echo through their bones. Rachel's stomach dropped to the saddle.

[*Rainor! What's going on? Mother?*]

[*Raiza, stay as still and as quiet as you can!*] Her mother advised her in a commanding tone.

Aryn was preparing his bow, Rik had his sword ready, and Lea and Sage followed Rik's lead bringing their attention to the direction the chilling sound had come from.

Surprisingly, something jumped at Rik from behind on his right and caught him off guard as claws and teeth tore through his right thigh. He swung downward with a mighty blow but the creature dodged the blade and readied itself for another attack. Lea, who had been facing the other direction when the beast struck, was now turned toward it ready to strike. Rainor tried to edge forward to help Lea, but Aryn cut him off and loosed an arrow directly into the beast's skull. It stopped mid-leap to crumple to the ground in death. Another creature lunged from the right of the group tearing a wound into the flank of Aryn's horse, a dapple grey named Rida. It whinnied in agony and reared up, but Aryn was able to steady himself as Sage turned and plunged his sword into the foul creature's side.

[*Expect one more! They travel in threes!*] Rik urgently sent through the group's minds between waves of pain.

Rachel's eyes were wide with panic and her mind was frantic.

[*Rainor, look out!*] Sage warned him just in time as the third beast leapt toward the front of Rainor's horse with his eyes locked on Rainor. Rainor froze. It wasn't the first time he had encountered these beasts, but it was the first time he was tortured into direct communication with one of them.

{*Kill…. Kill… Destroy!*} The chilling words were the beast's only consideration. They did not kill to eat or for any greater purpose. They were killing machines hell bent on destruction. They had been created from foul magic over a hundred years prior, but no one knew their original purpose. Sage was able to deal the final death blow, much to the relief of Rainor, as he shook his head and blinked away the mental connection. Three jackoyts, as they were called, were now dead. The group gathered around Rik whose injuries were the most severe.

"Rachel, please see to healing Aryn's horse if you are able," Eleese directed as she and Rainor helped Rik onto the ground.

Rachel dismounted and closed her eyes to step around the dead jackoyt. She had taken one look at it before all three were killed and did not ever want to see another one. Its limp form lay in a pool of thick, dark purple blood. Its small, yellow eyes now looked dull, and its mouth full of teeth was gaping open with its tongue to the side. She was sure to have nightmares of that face.

Rachel was shaking and still in shock over how calm everyone else seemed to be but focused herself on healing Rida. Aryn held the horse's head and stroked her nose to calm her. As Rachel's hands were placed on the horse, she side-stepped and shifted briefly then seemed to calm down. While Rachel worked, Eleese was tending to Rik. Aryn helped Sage drag the bodies of the jackoyts to some underbrush. After about an hour, both Rik and Aryn's horse were feeling good as new.

The sun had risen and the forest took on the calming effect Rachel had felt before on the day she arrived in Geerda. Sage offered to help Lea clean the blades that had ended the creatures' lives. Aryn strode back over to his horse and looked over Rachel's work. He said nothing but patted Rida's rump in satisfaction.

Rachel sighed and rolled her eyes. *Not even a 'thank you'.*

They each had a small bit of bread and some water before they were back in the saddles to continue on. The rest of the journey was just as Rainor had predicted, much more enjoyable. They could feel the warmth of the morning sun and encountered no further trouble.

Eleese quietly guided Rachel through some inner healing steps for her own thoughts and to strengthen her mind along with her ability to communicate between others' minds as well. Rainor was fairly quiet and Eleese could tell he was troubled by his encounter with the jackoyt. She paused with Rachel's training to speak to him.

[*Rainor, talk to me,*] she silently prodded him.

[*I'm not sure I can. Mother, it was more than just words that played in my mind ... it was as if it projected previous visions of killing and mutilation right into my soul. I feel so dark inside right now ... it's hard to explain,*] he returned to her.

[*I am truly sorry you had to endure such a thing.*]

[*When I close my eyes, I still see it. Is there anything you can do? Is there some sort of healing I can undergo?*]

[*Let me try once we get to our next stop. Until then, try to keep your mind on helping your sister. She looks as if she could use some rest and some reassuring as well.*] Eleese softly smiled toward Rachel as she ended her private conversation with Rainor. [*Raiza, how are you holding up?*]

[**Quite honestly, I am not sure I will ever want to sleep for fear of those ... things ... sneaking into my dreams!**] she confessed with a shudder, not caring that it was not a private thought.

[*I will attempt a healing on you both when we stop.*] the concern was evident in Eleese's shared private thoughts to her children, but she showed no outward signs of it.

No one else felt the need for conversation during the majority of the ride. After several hours, Rachel began to recognize the specific area as the place she had originally encountered the bushkins. She was thrilled when she could hear subtle clicking noises in the near distance. "Rainor, do you think we could stop? I am hoping to show the bushkins my new talents. Maybe I can heal … what did you call her? 'Itty'?"

"*Itsy* … and yes, I believe we should stop as well. Do you agree, Mother?" Rainor called out to Eleese who was just around the road to the left.

"Yes, I agree. I don't think, after what Raiza has told us, Otni would ever forgive me if we failed to stop and give Rachel a second chance to heal his daughter," she said with a raised eyebrow and a laugh.

They rode only a short distance farther to the mound of the bushkins and found a good place to set up camp. It was nearly supper time. Shortly afterwards, the bushkins were greeting everyone, and Sage and Lea produced a small treat for them all.

"Bushkins are quite fond of ghost-flower berries. Sage and I came across several bushes shortly before we left the jackoyts. At least *some* good came of that ordeal!" Lea smiled and passed out the fruit.

"Were those the bushes with the clear flowers?" Rachel asked.

Rik spoke up. "Yes, the berries are early this year ... the flowers are clear when wet and white when dry. The morning dew gives them their ghostly appearance," he explained as the bushkins purred with excitement.

A fire was started and a stew prepared with a large rabbit Aryn and Rik had captured along with some root vegetables they had packed along and some wild mushrooms from the bushkins. Rik, Aryn, and Sage finished setting up some tents and securing the horses while Lea and Rachel were entertained by the bushkins.

When Otni and Itsi came over to Rachel, she was overjoyed to show them that she could heal Itsi properly. The girl danced with delight when Rachel was done. It took only a short time and did not leave Rachel drained as it had when she healed Aryn's horse. Otni bowed to her in appreciation then patted his own head and looked at Rachel, giving her permission to pet him. She gave him a little pet then scratched his head gently. He purred in response as she laughed.

Rainor was still feeling the effects of the jackoyts despicable nature, so he and Eleese distanced themselves from the group so she could attempt to rid her son of the darkness he felt.

She placed a blanket on the ground and instructed Rainor to lie down. She sat herself at the top of his head and started her healing process by filling her mind with tranquil thoughts. She gently placed her thumbs on his temples and let her other fingers settle on his cheeks. She sucked in a short breath as the vile images assaulted her subconscious. She forced the thoughts out of her mind as she focused sending images of peace and restoration to her son. Rainor's face twisted and contorted as if in pain, and she heard him groan. She opened her eyes in concern and released her gentle embrace. "Are you alright?"

"I feel as if my thoughts were being scraped out of me. I'm not sure we should continue," he looked up at her with some remorse. "I'm sorry, Mother; I know you're only trying to help."

Eleese leaned over and kissed his forehead before rising and offering him her hand to help him to his feet.

"It was worth a try, so thank you," he managed a weak smile through his now throbbing headache. They went back to join the group, and Rainor's thoughts immediately went to Rachel.

[*Mother wasn't able to help me ... but maybe she can do something for you,*] he glanced her way when he mentally spoke to her.

[*I will ask her after she has had some time to relax. She looks quite weary ... there must have been quite a bit of damage in there. I feel terribly for you.*]

[*Oddly enough, just your voice in my head is somehow soothing, like cool water over a burn. I wonder ... maybe after you seek Mother's healing, you could try something on me. I'll ask her thoughts while we eat.*] His headache was already waning slightly.

The meal was nearly ready after an hour of simmering, and it smelled delicious. Rainor sat next to his mother with Rachel and Sage at one end of the cooking fire, while Aryn, Lea, and Rik sat at the other end. Bushkins crowded in between and around them all. Stew was passed around, and Sage pulled out a flagon of elven wine from his pouch with a sly grin. Rainor occasionally translated conversations between the travelers and the bushkins as they enjoyed each other's company.

Eleese was looking much less weary now and Rachel quietly asked her, "How did things go with Rainor?"

She sighed and glanced in his direction, shaking her head to indicate it had not gone well.

"Is there anything I can do? Could I try once you're done with my mind?" Rachel asked.

"No, I fear that your mind will be damaged in the process. You've still so much to learn. What Rainor has experienced reeks of an ancient foul magic. It has been a very long time since I have seen anyone affected in such a way," she said quietly with a look of concern washing over her features.

It was the first time Rachel saw evidence of her mother's softer side. She might need to put on a brave face for the others, but for her son and daughter, she could allow a moment of transparency. "We can certainly try to calm your mind though; I should have better luck with you since your experience wasn't so blatant."

With that, the ladies excused themselves briefly. As she had predicted, Eleese was able to easily rid Rachel's mind of the trauma, putting her at ease. She could still remember everything that had occurred, but it wasn't nearly as mortifying to think about. They returned to the fire and resumed their seats. Rachel smiled at Rainor and touched his hand as he reached across for some of Sage's wine.

The stew was eaten and more logs were added to the fire. It danced and crackled as the flames consumed the new fuel. The bushkins brought out small musical instruments and played for the group, dancing and clicking rhythmically to everyone's delight. It was a wonderful way to finish out their day.

Before they each went off to their tents, Rachel pulled Rainor aside. "I want to try to heal your mind, despite our mother's concerns." He looked away. "It will be fine," Rachel said. "If I feel anything is wrong, I'll stop." She moved around to face him. "But I feel I have to try."

She had convinced him. He took a deep breath and sat down on a nearby stump so she could begin. She was not completely sure where to begin, but closed her eyes and placed her forehead against his as she reached for his hands.

Instantly, she saw the horrid images he was being subjected to and it made her skin crawl. Her stomach lurched. She forced herself to continue. She swallowed hard, trying to keep her dinner down. She struggled to project images of happier thoughts: thoughts of sunsets, flowers, flavors she remembered, sweet smells, images of the happy times with the Mills, anything she could think of.

Suddenly, she thought of the moment she had realized Rainor was her brother. It flashed to the forefront of her mind – the pure comfort she had experienced when he spoke to her with his inner voice. A hole in her heart had been filled by his existence.

[*THERIN!*] Their shared inner name came to both of them in such a rush of power that she had to step back. Rainor smiled at Rachel as she grinned back at him realizing they had banished the oppressive atrocities from Rainor's mind. Rachel blinked away unshed tears and both had to calm their rapid breathing.

They ran to their mother to share the news with her. She placed her hand on Rainor's face and closed her eyes; she could feel the tranquility his mind now possessed. She gave Rachel a stern glance for disobeying. Rachel squirmed at the silent reprimand, but it was worth it when Eleese's features softened as she embraced them both.

"You truly share something very unique," she whispered to them before they parted ways toward their tents.

TRAVEL DAY ELEVEN

Lea was awake just before dawn and stepped out of the tent she and Rachel shared to go hunt. The forest was calm and the morning more quiet than normal. She soon returned, poking her head in the tent to check on Rachel. She had a dove for each of them in hand. She noticed Rachel had awakened. The sun was barely beginning to make its appearance, and Rachel smiled at Lea, feeling more revived and refreshed than she had in a long time.

"Good morning, my friend. Someone sure looks as if they slept well!" Lea laughed as she backed her head out of the tent and began preparing the morning fire for the doves.

Rachel came out to join her, "Yes! Whatever it was that happened when I attempted healing my brother seems to have worked on me as well. I feel so at peace this morning and so full of hope for my foster brother, Jon. Oh, Lea, you'll love him; he is such a special part of my life."

"I'm sure I will," replied Lea, dusting off her hands.

"Good morning, ladies," Rik greeted them with a smile as he joined Lea in preparing their breakfast. He brought out some sweet bread with honey and some dried fruits to go with the doves, raising his eyebrows to Lea to make sure she approved of the pairing.

She smiled and gave him a nod as she propped several long pieces of wood across the fire, each with a small skewered bird. As the smell wafted around camp, it brought others out of their tents until everyone except Sage had come to sit by the fire.

"I wonder why Sage isn't up. He's usually the first to the fire when there is food to be eaten," Rainor said with a chuckle. Rik offered to go check on him, but found he was not in the tent he shared with Rainor. Rik came back to the fire and asked Rainor if Sage had been there when he woke up.

"Yes, he was snoring when I came out to the fire. He can't be far. He must have needed some … alone time," he attempted not to laugh but failed.

After a while, the birds were taking on a golden brown skin and the friends were eager to dig in. They wondered where Sage was. He had not made it back yet. Eleese asked Rik and Aryn to make a quick circle around camp to see if they could locate him.

Soon, the three of them came back, Sage in his normal, relaxed mood laughing about the frustration apparent on Rik and Aryn's faces for having to search him out. They couldn't stay mad for long though. He had found more ghost-flower bushes and wild mushrooms to leave for the bushkins. Rachel and Lea were impressed with his thoughtfulness.

Breakfast was finished and camp cleaned up before the group presented the bushkins with their additional treats. They mounted back up and got on their way to the Twin Trees to meet up with Forrin. They wasted no time and arrived to see Forrin, Breeze, and three horses.

"Chestnut!" Rachel exclaimed as she put her hand on her heart. She was so happy to see her friend safe, with her original gear neatly packed and on his back.

"He came a running past my home the other night and stopped right where you had tied him the morning we met. I checked him over, no signs of injury. But I feared for your safety until this darling came to us with the news of your pending arrival. I'm glad to see you're alright," Forrin gave Rachel a small bow.

"Oh, Forrin, Thank you! Thank you for everything!" [*Can I tell him of the bond we share?*] she asked Rainor and the group.

[*Let's just keep it a secret for now,*] Rainor said back with all seriousness. He knew there may come a time when knowing less would be to Forrin's advantage if he were to be questioned.

[*Ok, but I may require an explanation for your expression later.*] She didn't understand. Forrin was her friend. *Why can't I tell him my good news?*

[*In due time,*] was his only reply, so Rachel let it go.

They spent a short amount of time visiting with Forrin who was in total awe of the elves. Rainor and Breeze made plans for her to take the horse Rachel had been riding back to the village and transferred the other gear she had to Chestnut. She was relieved to find everything in order, including the money from the sale of the falcon.

Thanking Forrin once more before mounting her horse, Rachel told him to pass along the thanks to Brondi and a hello to their children, promising she would be back to visit them again someday.

The level road ahead was easy to travel for the horses but the sun and lack of trees through this area made the group feel heavy and sticky. The Alexander Plains stretched across the middle of the island between Geerda and the base of the Conner Mountains. The terrain was dry with sagebrush and desert flowers. Crickets chirped until the group got close, silencing their song, even if just for a moment. Small rodents and an occasional lizard would cross their path but for the most part, they encountered no one.

It was an easy day, but a long day. Camp was set up in the open, so they opted not to light a fire. Aryn, Rik, and Rainor took shifts to guard the others during the uneventful night.

Rachel lay awake for a short time, thinking about her little brother, Jon. Wouldn't it be nice if she could communicate with him in the elven way? *Soon, Jon. I'll be back with you soon ... hang on.*

TRAVEL DAY TWELVE

Morning came with uncharacteristically warm temperatures for spring. The group didn't want to delay, so they packed up camp rather quickly and resumed their trek over the plains.

Conversations were light and dinner was eaten on the go. With no place to be seen for shade, the riders decided the slight mid-day breeze from their continued pace was more comfortable than sitting in the hot sun.

The dust played no favorites, covering the friends equally as they plodded along. Rachel kept her sights on the road ahead of them, squinting through the sun's brilliance. Since there was no scenery to speak of, the trip felt mundane, although the terrain did hold a certain beauty of its own. The ruddy qualities of the sandstone surrounding them made her feel even warmer than she actually was.

Daylight finally slipped behind them, creating long shadows that crept ahead. The shadows seemed to beckon them further but the group alternated their pace to keep the horses comfortable, and by dusk, they had stopped for the night. Conversations were held to a minimum as the weary travelers' minds thought of nothing but sleep.

TRAVEL DAY THIRTEEN

The next morning, they pressed the horses on through the endless monotony. A welcome sight ahead was a small group of trees, and they stopped nearby for some dinner in the shade before continuing.

Eleese had a friend that lived in a large home near the base of one of the smaller mountains and hoped they could reach her home before nightfall. She told the others about her friend, Cathryn Sutherlin, as they rode.

"We were once very close, but have not had as much contact over the years as I would have liked. I'm certain that Cathryn will let us stay the night at her manor. Her husband had been commissioned for several art pieces at the palace and had been quite successful, so their home is large and beautifully decorated. Their stables will be a welcome respite for the horses as well. When Cathryn's husband had passed away, she chose to continue living in the large manor with their two boys, having saved up plenty of money over the years to keep the hired staff and themselves comfortable. I hope that is still the case.

"The boys are close to your ages," Eleese said, glancing at Rainor, Rachel, Sage and Lea. "The last time I saw them, they were little terrors though – rough, rugged, human boys; I am curious as to their outcome."

The afternoon passed with little event, making another learning opportunity for Rachel as her mother helped her hone her new-found skills. They mostly worked on inner peace and private and shared mental communications. Rachel's mind had apparently had enough tranquility as it skid off course from her lesson and jumped to the story the old fisherwoman had told at the tavern in Brenton.

"What could have caused bursts of bright colors in the sky many years ago over Geerda?" Rachel blurted out.

After some discussion back and forth to narrow down what the time frame could have been, Eleese decided it must have been Desaree's visit to their village. "Desaree and I had enjoyed the light shows the village elders used to perform when we were children. Therek had some of the powders that create the effect. He launches them into the air then lights them on fire with his talents, creating quite a beautiful display. Maybe someday we will again have cause to celebrate in such a way," Eleese told Rachel with a faraway look in her eye.

Soon afterwards, Cathryn's home could be seen up ahead. It rested on a low hill and had a long path from the main road to the front door. The path was lined with large boulders that ended in a circular space at the front of the manor. Cactus grew in neatly planted gardens and lanterns had been lit along the path. Obviously, Cathryn's comfortable status had not changed.

The group dismounted their horses as a stableman greeted them and a doorman stepped out of the front entry. He greeted them and asked for their names and cause for visit. Eleese stepped forward and explained to him that she was an old friend of Lady Cathryn and gave him the information he requested.

She motioned to the others to wait as the doorman had her follow him to the manor. He showed her to a sitting room to the left of the front entry and went to retrieve Cathryn. In only a moment, Eleese could hear soft but hurried footsteps outside the room. The door was flung open and Cathryn glided across the small room to embrace her friend.

Cathryn was a simple beauty with a curvy frame and a warm smile. Her long, wavy, brown hair had a touch of gray which brought out her soft, green eyes. "Oh, Eleese! I have missed you!"

"I have been thinking of you often, Cathryn. Please forgive my appearance; we have been riding through the plains."

"Don't mind that. What brings you here? You are just in time for a late supper. Please join us!"

"I don't want to be a burden or intrude if you have company, but you see ... it isn't just me. I'm afraid I have need of lodging for several ..." Eleese fidgeted with the ends of her hair, much like Rachel would do. She didn't want to impose, especially after such a long time apart and with no warning.

"Nonsense, Eleese! You are always welcome, and there is plenty of room. Even with my boys here to visit as well. They arrived yesterday and will be thrilled to see you again. You won't believe how they have grown. Now, how many are you traveling with? Let me just go tell my staff to make the preparations."

Eleese gave her a headcount, a smile, and another hug. She came back outside to speak to the others. She took a brief moment to speak to Aryn privately, which Rachel thought was curious but said nothing, assuming it had something to do with their security. Aryn seemed tense, but not overly so. Arrangements were quickly made and horses secured in the stables after a thorough rub down and some oats. Each guest was shown to their room with a basin of hot water for freshening up and more food was prepared.

The men, Rik, Rainor, Sage, and Aryn were done freshening up before the ladies, so they joined their hostess and her sons in the dining room. Introductions were made. Cathryn's older son, Logan, was very outgoing, six feet tall with sandy brown hair and the same shade of green eyes as his mother. He was already, at twenty-two years old, successful in his trading business in Brenton. Her younger son, Treyton, also quite outgoing and friendly, stood two inches taller than his brother and was enormously muscular. Their hair color was the same but Treyton had blue eyes and a neatly trimmed beard. He lived in Dahlon and oversaw the making of the weaponry for the military training post in Traither. Both young men got along well with the newcomers.

When the ladies came into the dining room, one by one the men turned their attention toward them. Once again, introductions were made on the ladies' behalf. They all chose to dress in gowns Cathryn had loaned them and their hair had been done up in loose, stylish, braids and buns.

Rainor's eyes were immediately drawn to Lea; she was stunning in a fitted, deep burgundy gown that draped easily over her lean frame. He nudged Sage, who had been in conversation with Logan, as they both turned to take in her beauty.

It was obvious to Eleese that Lea was slightly uncomfortable. She had never worn a gown like this, usually opting for a loose flowing top and leggings, but she wore it well. Eleese wore a silvery blue gown with grace and ease, looking every bit the noble-woman. Rachel, who owned a few gowns of her own, was more comfortable than Lea but, like Lea, preferred a tunic and leggings as well. She swept into the room last and had on a sage green gown that was fitted on top and flowed out to a full skirt. For the first time in her life, she felt worthy of the attention the men now showed her; after all, she was a princess. Even with that fact now known to her, she blushed slightly as she noticed them gaping at all three of them.

"Ladies, may I be the first to compliment your attire this evening," Logan said with a low bow.

Rachel thought she caught Aryn rolling his eyes, but he quickly composed himself. The ladies smiled and nodded in thanks. Treyton and Logan led the ladies, one on each arm, to the table and the rest of the men joined them.

The meal was served as Eleese told Cathryn the reason for their journey. "Now that Raiza has returned to us, we have a renewed hope for the future. We must find a way to bring Stephan down."

Rachel interjected with her own side of the story as Cathryn and her sons pledged to help in any way they could. "I may not know what to do, or how to do it ... but finding out that my life was meant for so much more ... it just means so much that all of you are willing to help me."

It was decided halfway through the first course, a creamy vegetable soup, that Logan and Treyton would accompany them to Brimley. Neither of them was expected back home for some time. The second, and main, course was roast venison with small, red potatoes. It was such a hearty meal that

Rachel wasn't sure she could make it to the final course, dessert. When the servants took their plates and brought out the dessert, Rachel was instantly intrigued. Maybe she would change her mind. Small, silver bowls were brought out to each guest with a pale yellow content that Rachel had never seen before. The bowls were chilled and frosty in appearance. Next, each guest was given a steaming flagon of honey-colored liquid.

"Chilled lemon and warm, honeyed brandy," announced one of the servers.

"It's my sons' favorite way to eat a meal," Cathryn said with a smile. "We only have it on the rare occasions that both of them come for a visit, such as now."

"Too bad we have to share; I won't get my normal three bowls, huh, Logan?" Treyton teased as Logan furrowed his brow at the comment.

Rachel and the others had never had such an interesting treat. "There is a storage room behind my cellar that stays very cold most of the year, and we discovered that the plates and bowls we had been storing down there always had frost on them, so now we use it to chill certain desserts or drinks for the novelty of it."

Everyone agreed it was quite unique. With the meal finally completed, and everyone enjoying the last of their brandy, the two human men excused themselves to prepare for their departure with the elves, Rachel, and Rainor.

Cathryn was a wonderful hostess and now friend to everyone at the table. Her sons would be a great help to the party in their future endeavors, after they got Rachel back to her foster family. They fully intended to stay in Brimley for an extended time, plotting their next move to dethrone King Stephan. They would help to plan Rachel's part in those efforts after things had settled with the Mills.

It was getting late when Logan and Treyton joined the group in the sitting room. They were anxious for morning but wanted to spend some more time with their mother before their departure. Originally, the men had planned on staying with her for two weeks, but had only been there two days. Pulling her aside, Treyton asked, "Are you certain you're not too upset at us for leaving you, Mother?"

She replied sternly to both of her sons, "You boys don't understand the gravity of this situation with Rainor and Rachel. Learn whatever you can from Eleese and the others on the rest of this journey. Now, more than ever, you must listen to me.

I will be fine here and know that you will help your new friends to rid this land of that monster that calls himself 'King'... and while you're at it," she leaned in to continue, "break his witch of a mother too."

The men looked at their mother in shock, never having heard her speak in such a way.

"I'm sorry, but you have no idea what that woman has gotten away with, the horrible things she is suspected of doing to our friend, Eleese, and her husband's family." She displayed a flash of anger then smoothed her features into a smile as she rose to join the others and motioned to her sons to do the same.

After some light conversation Aryn stood, bowed to Cathryn, and excused himself to retire for the evening. Eleese glanced his way as he exited the room and gave a slight nod. Soon after, the rest of the travelers followed suit. They had planned an early breakfast then to be on their way.

"I am most grateful to you, Cathryn. Your kindness has touched my heart," Eleese thanked her friend as she retired for the evening.

Rachel again saw Eleese as less of a warrior and smiled at her mother's more tender side.

"Anything for a dear friend such as you. Keep my boys safe and use them to their full potential," Cathryn winked with a half-smile, fighting back her emotions.

Merri Gammage

TRAVEL DAY FOURTEEN

Breakfast consisted of boiled eggs, fruit, and glazed rolls with tea. Rachel sat between Treyton and Cathryn as they ate, Treyton asking Rachel all about her home and life before her journey. She was happy to talk to the two of them, entirely at ease with this family. It wasn't until the topic of Lane came up that she felt her comfort level shift. Treyton seemed intent on finding out if she would go back to Lane after things had settled in the next few days.

Rachel suddenly remembered her time with Eric from early in her trip and how he had so quickly become enamored with her. Was it happening again? She was going to be spending at least the next few days with this man and did not want to give him the wrong impression.

[*Rainor, help me out here.*] She silently clued him in to her discomfort.

[*Rachel, just accept it. You have an effect on human males ... Mother does too ... something about your healing abilities I think,*] he replied with an impish grin in her direction.

[*Really? You can't be serious.*]

[*Oh, I can, and I am. Ask her.*]

"Rachel? Rachel, more?" Treyton cut into her thoughts. She had missed the fact that he was offering her more tea.

"Oh, no. No, thank you. I'm sorry. I must have drifted off for a moment. I apologize," she turned to her mother and asked if she could take a moment of her time. The two excused themselves and left the room.

"Mother, because of my talents, Rainor said I have some effect on human men. Is this true? I seem to be attracting unwanted affections." She picked at her fingernail and chewed her lower lip.

"Oh, Raiza. Do you not know how stunningly beautiful you are? You seem to doubt that any young man could find you desirable ... but yes, there is some truth to your brother's words." She shrugged. "Remember when I told you that Jon clung to you because of your then unknown abilities? Somehow, he can sense that you can help him. It is no different with men you will encounter, except for the fact that they may not need healing. But take great comfort from your aura. They see a beautiful and kind young lady and feel a soothing comfort in your presence; they can't help but fall for you," she said with a bit of a laugh as Rachel took it all in.

"It's not going to make traveling any easier," she said with a wry smile.

[*Things could be worse. At least these young men are honorable and not bad looking either ... but if it makes you more comfortable, just stay closer to your other kind: Rainor, Rik, Sage, Lea and Aryn,*] Eleese offered silently as they rejoined the others.

Aryn ... she thought as her eyes rolled.

Breakfast dishes were cleared away, servants had prepared the horses, and everyone said their goodbyes and thanks to Cathryn as they prepared to depart. Eleese took up the lead once more with Rainor and Logan directly behind her, Treyton, Rachel, and Aryn next, and Sage, Rik and Lea bringing up the rear. Rachel sighed at the thought of who flanked her. *This should be entertaining,* she thought sarcastically. Rainor and Logan seemed to have enough to talk about, and Rachel could sense something between Sage and Lea that she couldn't pinpoint but noticed that they seemed friendlier with each other than they had previously. She wondered if it was simply the great rest they had gotten the prior night. Rik happily joined in their conversation. Aryn was his normal quiet self, but Rachel couldn't get Treyton to shut up. There was one advantage to that though – time passed by quickly that morning.

They came upon a small creek and some low bushes about an hour past midday and decided to stop and rest the horses. While they ate dried fruits and cheeses, they visited with each other casually until the sounds of several horses and a carriage in the distance alerted them to other travelers. Up until now, they had only come across the occasional loner and hadn't worried about whom they shared this more secluded road with.

Eleese quickly tied the horses together, as if they were being led with no riders and sent private messages to Rik, Lea, Sage, and Aryn to drop out of sight. She instructed Rainor and Rachel to tell any inquisitors that they were working for Lady Cathryn, transporting goods to Brimley with her sons. Rainor passed along the plan to Logan and Treyton who easily caught on as to why. If they had been caught traveling with elves, it may spell trouble.

Soon enough, the wagon sped into view and slowed at the approach of the four friends. It was an elaborate coach from Brimley Palace with several soldiers escorting it. The lead soldier came forward to question the group, and Logan stepped forth. Treyton nodded toward the soldier, recognizing him from prior weapons purchases, and they carried on with little concern. The soldier signaled to the others that there was no danger for them. As the coach passed, Rachel glanced in the window to see two beautiful young women with dark hair and kind faces.

"Those are Princess Sarah's daughters," Logan whispered to her. "Emily and Eva – aren't they beautiful?"

Rachel could tell he had made their acquaintance before. "Yes, quite so. They appear kind as well. Is that the case?"

"Oh, yes, quite perceptive. I've met them a time or two … they may make good allies. I believe Sarah and Desmond were quite close …" he replied as he watched them travel out of sight.

"All clear!" Treyton called to the others.

"Cousins?" Rachel looked to Rainor as it sunk in. Sarah was Stephan's younger sister;

therefore, Emily and Eva were indeed their second cousins.

The elves rejoined them, and they were back on their way. Eleese was curious as to what the girls would be doing so far from the palace but said nothing to the others.

The formation switched up so that Rik was now in the front, Logan, Eleese, and Treyton next, Rachel and Rainor in the center, and Aryn, Lea, and Sage to follow. The dynamic of conversations had changed now. The afternoon sun beat down on the riders, and they were more focused on the plans for the future, along with some historical teachings from Eleese. Treyton and Logan were listening intently along with Rachel and Rainor. Sage and Lea seemed to be in their own world. Now and again, Aryn would ride up next to Rachel then hang back as soon as she glanced his way. She smiled at him more than once, but got nothing in return.

[*How can someone so handsome never manage to smile?*] she asked Rainor.

He turned to her with a puzzled look, having not been paying attention to anything but the conversation ahead of them. [*And who would that be?*]

[*Never mind, it's not important,*] she shrugged, not caring that most everyone else could hear.

Just to tease her a bit, he flashed a smile at her [*Just in case you were referring to your handsome brother.*] Then he winked at her.

Rachel blurted out a laugh before covering her mouth with her hand and apologizing to her mother for the interruption. [*No, Rainor, I was NOT referring to you,*] she shot back with a stifled chuckle.

The day wore on. The steady rhythm of the horses and the hum of conversation ahead of her, mixed with the heat of the late afternoon, made Rachel drowsy. She wondered when they would stop again but knew it would most likely be dusk before they would dismount. She tried to keep herself awake by taking in her surroundings. The area seemed familiar somehow, though she hadn't remembered traveling this way before. The plains were dotted with more trees now, and the road they were on became rockier as they wound closer to the small mountains to their right. Rachel had lived at the base of these mountains growing up, but farther – Northeast where even more pines grew.

They continued on through a very small village of people who Eleese knew to be friendly to elves, who advised them of a cave farther down the road where they could sleep. After another few hours, they found the cave near the road. It was large enough to house all nine of them comfortably for the night. The dry, rocky ceiling was at least fifteen feet above, and they set about making a fire near the cave entrance. The horses' gear was removed and they were tied for the evening in a grassy area nearby with some small apple trees.

Aryn picked an apple for his horse, and then offered one to Rachel who stood nearby softly speaking to Chestnut. She had missed his companionship from when it was just the two of them. She took the apple from Aryn with a nod and noticed how quickly he jerked his hand away when her finger grazed his palm. She met his gaze, but he turned to sit by the fire. Shaking her head, she turned back to Chestnut and gave him the apple.

"Whatever do you suppose *that* was about?" she whispered to the horse. "He certainly is odd … more handsome than anyone I have ever seen, but odd," she admitted quietly as she placed her forehead against Chestnut's nose. He nudged her gently. After a few more pats and kisses for Chestnut, Rachel joined the others for some food.

Lea came around from a tree with several fish and announced that there was a small lake just beyond where they camped. Rachel was impressed at Lea's ability to obtain fish or game in a matter of moments. The roasted fish was a nice change.

After supper had been eaten, they decided to go to the lake Lea had mentioned for a swim before sunset. The ladies sat on the rocks at the water's edge dangling their feet in the soothing water. The men were a bit more adventurous, stripping down to their undergarments to jump in. The water, quite deep in some parts, allowed the men to dive down deep before exploding from the depths gasping for breath. Lea was asking Eleese about some berries she had found nearby when Sage jumped into the water next to her, drenching one side of her. Eleese and Rachel's eyes widened with shock, fully expecting Lea to be angry. Instead, she laughed joyously, dropped the berries, and jumped in to dunk his head as she tackled him. He came up sputtering and laughing and grabbed her face, pulling it toward his. Their foreheads came together and something flashed across both their faces.

[*Moorin*]

[*Soreen*]

In that moment, their inner names were shared, bonding them for life. Eleese was fully aware of what had just transpired, but Rachel looked on in surprise as Sage sealed the bond with a passionate kiss.

Rainor, who was several feet away, also knew but turned from the scene closing his eyes in defeat. He had a desire budding for Lea, but knew now that they were not destined to be united. He secretly wished it wouldn't have been his best friend to have formed that bond with her, but he would have to accept it and at least try to be happy for them.

The elves, except for Aryn who had left just as the two bond-mates had kissed, cheered and congratulated the newly-bonded couple, even Rainor. Eleese then explained to Logan and Treyton, as Rachel listened in (even though she had guessed by that point, she wasn't sure she was correct).

Sensing Rainor's sudden shift in emotion, she nudged his thoughts [*You were hoping it would be you, weren't you?*]

[*Yes, but it was not meant to be. I will be OK with it in time; this is the way it should be.*] His assurances sounded like he was trying to convince himself more than his sister.

[*Is it always that easy?*] Rachel inquired.

[*Not always, but usually. Sometimes it can happen upon meeting someone soon after puberty or it can take years of knowing someone then suddenly happen. You might sense it happening, but it can take you by surprise as well ...*] Rainor's thought trailed off as he looked across the lake.

One by one, the travelers finished their fun in the water and began to head back to camp. The ladies stayed behind a few extra moments to wash their hair as the sun dipped near the horizon. As they gathered their things, Lea led them to the path she had taken earlier to pick some more berries to share around the campfire. They each filled their hands with the sweet, dark berries.

Rachel popped one into her mouth to taste-test it. A memory, long forgotten, filled her mind from when she was a toddler. Not only did she remember having eaten these berries before (though she remembered them being dried), but she had eaten them in that very spot. She couldn't explain it. Slowly, she turned in a circle as the visions of her past blasted her field of vision. She could see herself as a small child, out there alone in the snow, eating past-ripe, dried berries, crying from hunger and fear.

She began to shake, dropping to her knees as tears streamed down her cheeks.

Eleese and Lea stopped talking and Eleese glanced over to see her daughter drop down before the berry bush. She ran to her. Lea was close behind her.

"Raiza! What is it?" her mother demanded.

"It isn't the berries, is it?" Lea's concern was that she had been poisoned by them, seeing the purple juices that stained Rachel's hands.

"No ... I've been here, Mother," Rachel managed to gasp out. "When I was a small child, I was crying and all alone ... and so cold ... and then Dad, I mean Jack, scooped me up and wrapped me in a blanket. That's all I remember." By this time, she was fiddling with the ends of her hair, staining it, tears still streaking her face.

[*Rachel!*] Rainor's voice called to her with concern from the other trail. He could sense something was wrong.

[*She's over here,*] Eleese stood so Rainor could see where they gathered, through the trees.

Lea sat next to Rachel, gently rubbing her back while Eleese told Rainor what had transpired.

"Let's get her back to camp," Rainor suggested as he helped her up and hugged her to his side.

Rachel swiped her tears away as they made it back to sit by the campfire. Dusk had settled in and, after being in the water, the fire was comforting. Treyton rushed over to help Rainor get Rachel seated.

She relayed her experience to the rest of the group; it was a mixture of relief and frustration. She was relieved to have remembered what she had, but more questions flooded her mind, questions she may never get answered.

Rainor pulled Rachel closer, to Treyton's irritation. Oddly, Rainor caught Aryn glancing over and smirking at this.

"Please forgive me, everyone. I certainly did not intend on bringing down our good moods tonight, but that is the first memory I have had from before my life with the Mills." She looked around the group to find kindness and sympathy on their faces, most of them anyway; Rik was tending to the embers in the fire, and Aryn, like always, was back to cleaning his dagger.

"We've got berries," Lea sheepishly offered from a large bowl. That, at least, made Rachel smile.

Soon the mood was lighter and sleeping arrangements were set inside the cave. Except for Sage and Lea, who opted to share a common space, everyone spread out comfortably enough. Eleese and Rainor placed themselves to either side of Rachel. Rainor was mildly uncomfortable with Sage and Lea being in such close quarters but tried to push the minor jealousy from his mind. Sage was his best friend, basically a brother, and had bonded with his soulmate. Rainor should be happy for them. He was. It just wasn't comfortable to think about what they might be sharing with each other, not so far away, in the cave.

Rachel sensed Rainor's discomfort and couldn't help but feel for him.

[*Rainor, I know you are still awake. Can you clear up a couple questions I still have on this bonding thing between Sage and Lea?*] She could tell he wasn't completely annoyed with her question, but she thought she better choose her words carefully. [*Is there always a mutual bond? I mean ... is there ever a time where one person feels it and the other does not? Or can you choose to ignore the bond if you wanted to?*]

[*As far as I know, it is always mutual – since it is meant to be. I have never heard of it being one-sided. Although I suppose maybe it's possible to ignore. I have heard that if you try, it will be like ripping yourself apart. The deep connection that is made when bonding is more than say ... a human vow ... it is an entire blending of souls. I believe we have a different type of bond, but very similar, because we are twins. Remember how incomplete we both felt before finding each other? And now how complete we feel? I imagine it will be something like that – but on a different level.*] He was very patient in his explanation.

[*I think I understand now, thank you ... and I'm sorry to have brought it up again. Good night.*]

[*Actually, I think answering your questions has helped me to resolve some of my own issues with the whole thing. Let's get some rest.*] He rolled over.

Rachel felt much better than she had earlier and had a better understanding of things. She was glad her mother and brother were close by as she drifted off. Rachel dreamt of herself as a toddler. She could feel the cold of the snow around her and the hunger pains that cramped her small stomach. She was calling to someone, but they would not reply; it was Brock and Rebecca, the humans who had taken her in. She wondered where could they have gone; why had she been abandoned? Fear crept deep into her soul as her toddler-self struggled to understand what had happened. She felt an overwhelming sense of loneliness.

Rainor picked up on his sister's distress and reached out for her. He placed his hand gently on her arm. She woke slightly. "You were whimpering," he whispered.

"I was having a horrible dream of when I was lost and alone," she muttered and shivered slightly. Realizing she was safe and warm now, with family surrounding her, she smiled and fell back asleep.

Rainor remained awake for only a short time, until he was confident that his sister had settled back into sleep.

TRAVEL DAY FIFTEEN

Rachel was wedged between her brother and her mother, and she was sweltering. She carefully slid herself out from between them and decided to step outside the cave for some fresh air. It was still dark. She sat on a nearby boulder staring out at nothing. She could sense someone else's presence. She turned ever so slightly and caught sight of Aryn at the entrance to the cave, the dim glow of the moon highlighting his features. She heard him sigh, then he turned to go back in the cave.

Amazing, she thought to herself, half in appreciation of his physique, half sarcastically at the fact that he had not even acknowledged her. *Why do I care? Sure, he's good-looking. OK, maybe that's an understatement. But he has never been overly nice or even moderately social with me.* Still, she hoped he could at least show some courtesy eventually.

Rachel sat alone waiting for the sun to rise. She was in reflection of all that had happened up to this moment: leaving home, meeting new people, finding the bushkins, a twin brother, Geerda, her mother and grandparents, making new friends, learning she was a healer and a princess, almost getting killed by the jackoyts, remembering a small piece of her past, and now almost back home. Jon was the first one she thought of when she thought of home. Her heart leapt at the image of him in her mind. She couldn't wait to see him, hug him, and hopefully heal him. How happy that would make Jack and Mavis. Hopefully they would forgive her for leaving as she did. She allowed one stray tear to trace her cheek. She missed them all terribly. *One more day.* She collected her thoughts and padded silently back to the cave. The sun was just throwing its rays over the land.

The others began to stir after a short time. Rachel had started a small fire to warm some biscuits for everyone. They were a bit stale, not soft or fresh, but some warm steam from a pot of hot water would give them a more appealing texture. She found some tea stashed away as well, so she steeped some of the leaves and set out some dried fruit.

"We'll be crossing the Rune today," Eleese calmly told Rachel as she sat down with an empty mug extended toward the pot. Rachel carefully filled it with tea. The others joined them and Treyton took a seat next to Rachel asking how she slept.

"Well, and you?" she replied politely.

"A bit chilled, no extra body heat and all ..."

"Treyton! Enough, where are your manners?" his older brother glared at him from across the fire.

"What? I wasn't trying to imply ... well ... I wasn't ... never mind. It just wasn't as warm as in the tents the night before is all ..." he tripped on his words as he looked down, ashamed of what it must have sounded like. He truly meant nothing by it, but could understand why his brother thought otherwise.

Logan knew the feelings his brother had for Rachel even in the short time they had known her. The fact was he wondered if he had fallen for her himself. What wasn't to like? She was beautiful, petite yet strong, and at the same time vulnerable, not promised to anyone that he could tell, and the way he felt when she was near – comforted and peaceful – he could live with that. If only Treyton hadn't already confided in him of his feelings. Otherwise, she might have been fair game. Logan couldn't do that to his brother. He would remain silent unless she made advances toward him. He knew that was highly unlikely, but he could hope.

Sage and Lea were like lovesick puppy dogs but they weren't obnoxious about it and even Rainor smiled at how happy they seemed together. Rik and Aryn were pre-occupied with getting the horses ready and the gear packed up, always the responsible ones. After they ate, Rainor, Logan, and Treyton quickly joined them. Eleese and Rachel doused the fire and did one last check around camp to make sure they had everything. Treyton brought their horses to them and took Rachel aside to apologize again if his earlier comment made her uncomfortable.

"No, Treyton, I'm fine," she assured him. He assisted her into the saddle with one quick lift and they were on their way yet again.

Rik took the lead with Sage and Lea behind him, Rainor, Rachel, and Aryn next, and Logan, Eleese, and Treyton took up the rear. Rachel was feeling fortunate for this set up. She knew Sage and Lea's conversation would be light and upbeat, and she and Rainor could easily converse, and Aryn … well … she didn't mind the view. Logan, Eleese, and Treyton were going over some contacts the men had, delighted to find out Eleese also knew some of them or at least their families. They were confident they could spread the word about the twins' rightful place on the throne and their plans to defeat King Stephan without letting the word get to him. They would have to choose their allies carefully though.

The air was cooler this morning. Treyton had been right about that. There was a blanket of fog resting throughout the trees. They made their way cautiously through the lower mountain valley toward the Rune River. Slowly, they made sure there were no other travelers or unseen troubles to worry about. The sun was attempting to burn off the fog and Eleese was sure it would dissipate in another hour or so. She was right.

By midday, the group was passing through a meadow with the river in sight. The tall grasses, dotted with colorful wildflowers, swayed in the afternoon breeze. It had turned out to be a beautiful day.

They stopped for dinner, and Aryn and Lea scouted ahead for a good place to cross. The Rune was a large and fast-running river that sprawled out in some areas to a much more shallow and manageable body of water. This was not one of those areas.

Rachel took in the beauty of the meadow. It reminded her of the fields where her foster father kept his sheep. She missed her family terribly. Soon they would be reunited.

Aryn and Lea returned shortly and guided the group toward a bridge. "Eleese, did you know about the bridge here? It looks quite new ... wide enough for a carriage, I'm sure that one we saw came through that way," Lea informed her leader.

"No, I wasn't aware of that. We'll gladly use it to cross though; I was worried about our gear making it across those waters," she replied with relief.

Aryn and Eleese took the lead heading east toward the bridge. The rest fell into place randomly. If they traveled in twos, they could easily cross the slightly mounded bridge to the northern side of the Rune. The horses' hooves clopped out a hollow rhythm as they went. The bank was dotted with small shrubs and a river rat plunked itself into the water as the last of them filtered off the far side of the bridge. The road on the north bank split in two – one road appeared to stick close to the Rune to the northwest, the other to the northeast through the low mountains; this would be their path. The farther they progressed along the road, the denser the pine trees grew around them. The route was not an easy one. It became narrow and rocky to a point where they decided to go in single file. Eleese took the lead again, then Aryn, Rainor, Rachel, Rik, Logan, Treyton, Lea, and Sage.

Rachel breathed in the familiar scent of the hills and trees. She knew they were closer to her home. Conversations were kept to a minimum due to their formation. The horses' muscles tensed with each step as they maneuvered through the shale and uneven ground. Occasionally, Chestnut's hoof would *thunk* against a root or his footing would slip on the rocky terrain, but he continued on without protest.

As the sun began to cast long shadows ahead of them, the path broadened again. Rainor slowed his mount to position himself next to Rachel on the right. Treyton took the opportunity to catch up to Aryn's right (so he was directly in front of Rainor), while Logan moved up to Rik's side and Lea and Sage were content in the back. Treyton turned in the saddle so he was facing Rachel.

He smiled. "How does it feel to be returning home?"

"I'm hopeful that Eleese and I can heal Jon. After all, that was what I originally set out for, a healer for my brother. Little did I know there was *much* more in store for me!" she replied with an uneasy laugh.

"I'm here for moral support, if you should need a friend, unless you feel your *boyfriend* would become jealous," Treyton offered with a mischievous grin.

Rachel thought the statement was odd but was intrigued when she caught Aryn's expression. If his eyes could shoot arrows, Treyton would be dead. It didn't last; Aryn quickly turned his attention back to Eleese's lead. Rachel wasn't sure how to reply to Treyton but she didn't have to say anything. Logan spoke for her, again chiding his brother.

"Treyton, it is none of your business. Leave the poor girl alone. I'm sure she has plenty of 'friends' to lend her support. Besides, she is not obligated to tell you any more of her status with Lane," Treyton turned back around.

Rachel was shocked that Logan remembered Lane's name, let alone their 'status', as he put it.

[*I think someone has more than one admirer,*] Rainor cut into her thoughts with humor in his words.

[*I give up,*] she sighed back.

"We'll stop up ahead near that outcrop; it will provide some shelter from this breeze," Eleese's smooth voice interrupted.

Rachel had not noticed the chill in the air until her mother brought it to her attention. It was nearly dark and the temperature at the mountain base was cooler. She would relish the warmth of the fire and a good rest. This night would be her last on the open road.

Tomorrow, they would arrive at the Mills' and hopefully be welcomed when they got there. Her whole world had been turned around. How would Jack and Mavis respond to the news she brought? There was so much to tell.

The small outcrop of stone shielded the group from the breeze that was now blowing due west. Luckily, they were able to tuck themselves just out of its chilly grasp. Lea excused herself to go on a quick hunt and Sage followed. She stopped and turned to him with an apprehensive look. He cocked his brow with a tilt of his head, wondering what her sudden guarded behavior was all about.

[*I'm OK on my own, Soreen. I'll be careful,*] she tried to dismiss her actions, silently pleading with him to stay behind.

He was unsure why it mattered to her so much to be alone [*Moorin, what is it? I sense fear in you. What is going on?*] He questioned her with nothing but concern. The others just looked on or went about their business of setting up camp.

[*Sage, please,*] she begged him once more.

"Fine. Go. Be careful," he tersely replied and sulked back to the rest.

[*What was all that about?*] Rainor asked.

[*I'm not the least bit sure; it was like she was afraid of being alone with me out there. I don't like it Rai.*]

His friend was confused and hurt. Rainor didn't like it either. [*Rachel, can you find out what that was about? Something is not right here.*]

[*When she comes back, I will see what I can find out. The tension in the air is rather thick.*] Rachel hoped she could pull some answers from Lea. She had been completely fine until that moment; it was odd.

Moments later, the fire was crackling peacefully. Everyone had set up their tents and was enjoying some time out of the saddle. Lea crept back to camp with three large rabbits. She set them by Rik and quietly asked if he could prepare them for the fire. She glanced toward Sage, who was now beginning to scowl, then to Rachel with a look of distress.

She caught the hint from her friend. "Lea, could you come help me with my ... um ... bedroll?" Rachel asked as she dragged Lea by the arm to her tent.

"Thank you!" Lea sighed as they entered the tent Rachel and Eleese would be sharing.

"Excuse me, gentlemen," Eleese quietly stood and went to join Rachel and Lea. "What are you two up to? Are you OK, Lea?" she questioned with a stern gaze between the two.

"I don't know ..." Lea huffed as she sat down. "I knew this day would come, I just wanted more time to prepare myself ... more time to plan out how I would tell Sage ..." she told her friend and her leader with her head bowed.

"Are you already with child?" Eleese asked, approaching Lea.

"No! Oh, goodness, no. We haven't even ... well ... with everyone else around, we just didn't feel it would be appropriate. It's killing us, but no, not that," she said with a laugh.

"Then, what is it?" Rachel encouraged.

"It's my gift, my special skill ... you both have such a noble gift that you can share freely and be proud of. Mine is ... how do I explain it?" She pondered her own question for a long moment. The other two ladies looked on with anticipation. Then finally, "I'll just have to show you."

There in the tent, with Rachel and Eleese looking on in astonishment, Lea's body began to change. It took only a brief moment but was quite shocking to see. Lea's size shrunk considerably, then her knees popped and her joints turned backwards. Her arms withdrew some and her back bent forward. Her clothes slid off onto the floor.

Rachel wasn't sure if she wanted to look away or keep watching. Eleese had seen a shifter before, but they were rare in the village. She guessed that Lea was unaware of the others due to her uneasiness about her own abilities. Lea's face was the last to change. As her eyes slid back to the sides of her face and her nose elongated, her ears spread upwards, the teeth and whiskers finished off the transformation.

"Whoa," was all Rachel could manage to say. Before her eyes was a jack rabbit where her friend had been standing.

"I know. I don't know how Sage will react … and I feel ashamed sometimes, as this is how I am able to hunt so quickly. I hunt as one of them, whatever it is I'm after, or as a predator. It just depends on my mood. Sometimes I feel like it's unfair." The sadness was evident, even in Lea's new form.

To Rachel, it was unsettling to see a rabbit speak. Eleese rested her palm on Lea's soft fur. She fed Lea with feelings of confidence and acceptance. "I'm sure you have nothing to fear with Sage. He is your bond; he will understand. We are not naturally coupled to another if they would not compliment who we are and the same the other way." She couldn't help but give Lea's ear a light tug. The ladies shared a laugh. Rachel's came out more shocked sounding than the others.

My friend changes into animals … who would have thought it possible?

As quickly as she had changed into a rabbit, Lea was now changing back to her elven form. She got dressed and stretched with a few pops in her joints.

"Does that hurt?" Rachel wondered aloud, still in awe at what she had just witnessed.

"Not anymore. The first time it did, but with each new form, my body learns to adapt." She dismissed it with a shrug.

"Shall we?" Eleese motioned to the tent entrance and the three ladies went back to the fire. Eleese gave Lea a reassuring nod as she took Sage's hand and led him away to explain.

[*Lea is a shifter, but not sure how to break the news to Sage,*] Eleese explained to Rainor, who was looking at them expectantly.

[*Oh wow, that explains a lot ... he might just enjoy that talent!*] He sent back with a laugh.

"Everything alright?" Rik asked

"It will be," Eleese nodded.

Rachel was still in shock. That wasn't something you just got over in a couple minutes.

Sage and Lea returned to the fire. The rabbits were roasted and eaten and the rest of the fruit they had packed had been passed around. Sage sat quietly with a goofy grin on his face.

[*Did you hear?*] He asked Rainor.

[*Ha! Yes, I did. With your abilities to control water, mixed with hers to shift, I can only imagine what your children will come out like! You may end up with a school of fish!*] Rainor teased his friend as they began preparing to retire for the evening.

[*Good night,*] the thought whispered in Rachel's mind so quietly she wasn't sure who had sent it. It was similar to a thought you would have between being awake and falling asleep. She knew it wasn't her mother or Rainor. She glanced around but caught no one's eye. She knew it was a private thought, but responded out loud.

"Good night, everyone. Sleep well." Logan and Treyton eagerly replied first, then the others did as well except for Aryn, who merely nodded with a smile. A smile! *My goodness, he has dimples,* Rachel noted, as many butterflies suddenly took up residency in her gut. *Was the mystery message from him?*

TRAVEL DAY SIXTEEN

Rachel woke to the familiar clicking and jeering of a nearby jay. There were many of these birds close to her home and the sound normally brought her joy. Today, it did little to lighten her mood. They had slightly more than half a day's ride to reach the Mills'. She was filled with anticipation and angst.

Eleese sat up, feeling the sudden tension radiating off her daughter, and greeted her with a sleepy yawn. "Don't worry so. It will be alright, I have no doubts."

Rachel relaxed her tense shoulders very little at her mother's words. She sat up with her elbows resting on her knees. "I can't help but feel that something is wrong. I can't explain it but Jack and Mavis have never indicated directly how they feel about the elves. What if they are not willing to side with us? What if they turn us away? Or worse yet, turn us in? Maybe there is something else to explain this … feeling … in the pit of my stomach." There was agony in her questions.

"They love you. Do you not know this to be true? I have heard it in the stories you have shared with us. I am thankful that they found you and took you in. I have every confidence they will come around, maybe not immediately, but they will." Eleese had such a soothing nature about the way she spoke. It wasn't the words, as they were always matter-of-fact, but the serenity and confidence she emanated as she spoke them. It really did help Rachel relax. The two got dressed and joined the others, already at the fire.

Rachel sat next to Lea, who offered to braid her hair. As she did, she wove ribbons of blue and green throughout the strands, matching the outfit Rachel had chosen for the day. She wore deep doeskin-colored leggings with a cream tunic and vest of deep blue with green trim, and her tall riding boots. Lea wove an intricate pattern in Rachel's golden locks. The braid came together at the middle of her back. It was a traditional elven style.

Eleese was admiring Lea's nimble fingers. "I have never mastered that one, but it has always been a favorite of mine." She smiled warmly at the two.

Rainor, Sage, and Logan were discussing the prior night's discovery concerning Lea (with her permission) and wondering if her skills could somehow come in handy gaining access to the castle. She could hold her form for as long as she chose and had already agreed to help in any way she could. Several times during the men's conversation, Sage's eyes met with Lea's with a great sense of pride. Her gifts were truly rare and remarkable.

Rik and Treyton were off from the group in friendly competition, wrestling with each other in a game of upper body strength. Both men, incredibly well built, gave the other a great challenge. They continued on, Rik several years Treyton's senior, taunting then advising.

Aryn was nowhere to be seen. Rachel glanced around casually, not wanting to appear as if she was actively looking for him. His tent and gear were packed up and ready to put back on his horse, which was standing with the others, so she knew he was probably close.

"Ouch!" she gasped as Lea held her head still for the last part of the braid. "Why so rough?"

Lea just laughed. Rachel turned her attention back to Lea and Eleese's conversation, but her thoughts drifted again. His smile, those dimples, that body, kept creeping back into her mind. If only his personality matched the physical qualities! But, *No one is perfect*, she reminded herself. *Besides, even if he was more social, or even friendly, surely he wouldn't be interested in me.* She was a princess by right, but grew up in a small town as a sheep farmer's daughter. He was the head of the guard in Geerda. She felt she wasn't as beautiful as he was handsome. He would most likely already have a love interest back in Geerda, wouldn't he? She really knew nothing about him, except that she needed to stop her silly obsessing over him. *But that smile!*

"Rachel?" Lea put her hand on Rachel's shoulder snapping her out of her reverie.

"Oh! I'm sorry. I do that all too often. What were you saying?" she offered apologetically. Lea made a gesture to the others who were all preparing to leave. Eleese had picked up their tent, the horses were saddled and ready to go, the fire was out. Rachel closed her eyes and cringed at just how long she must have been wrapped up in her thoughts about Aryn. She rose to her feet. "Well, yes, let's be on our way then," she mumbled.

As they mounted up, Rachel offered to take the lead. She had been almost this far from home once before and felt confident she knew the way from there. There were few roads to contend with, mostly just hunting trails. She just had to stick to the main pathway from here. Rainor rode next to her, Eleese behind, then Lea and Sage, Logan and Treyton, and Rik and Aryn.

The sky was blue with only a few feathered clouds across it. The air felt cool but pleasant. Rainor did his best to keep Rachel talking, and keep her mind off her worries. They rode along through the pines for over an hour. Then the trees began to thin out again.

In the distance, Rachel could barely make out the old, crumbling barn that marked the edge of the Patterson farm, a long forgotten plot of land at the edge of Brimley Downs. For some reason, it was abandoned many years prior. Rumor was the ground would no longer yield crops. From the border of that property, it was 3 miles to the Mills' farm.

"Familiar territory?" Rainor asked quietly as he noticed Rachel's posture grow tense.

"Yes, it's less than an hour ride from that farm, there …" She pointed to the barn.

"Do you want to continue at this pace? Or shall we press ahead at a gallop, making a grand entrance?" he teased her lightly.

"Let's take it slowly; I'm not sure I want everyone descending on the Mills all at once. Poor Mavis hates surprises!" she declared with a sigh. She glanced over her shoulder at Eleese, "Once we arrive, maybe I should approach them on my own."

The five elves (including Rainor) nodded in agreement while Logan and Treyton offered to accompany her.

Rainor stifled a chuckle. Those two had indeed both fallen for his sister. They were both good men. He wondered what she would do; he didn't think she returned either's affections. He had a feeling there was someone else she was thinking about.

"I really feel this is something I need to approach on my own, but thank you, Logan. Thank you, Treyton." She smiled at them for the offer, but as she turned back in her saddle, she rolled her eyes.

"You let us know when to part ways, and we can await your return. We *will* respect your wishes," Rainor said loud enough for the rest of the group to acknowledge.

"Thank you. There is a tavern and an inn a mile and a half past the Patterson farm. They will take care of the horses and hopefully you should all feel welcome there."

"Brimley Downs. I've been here before, but it's been a while, I think I know the innkeeper there," remarked Logan.

"You know of him?" Rachel turned to him in surprise.

"I've known him for many years, if it is still 'Old Mathis' " he stated.

"Not likely 'Old Mathis' but probably his son. Mathis the second maybe? I would guess he is in his forties," She thought about it for a moment, not having seen him for some time.

Logan threw back his head with laughter, "No, no. That is the same one. I call him 'Old' because I met him when we were merely fourteen, and he nearly had a full beard back then. He is the same age as me, two and twenty," he said with a comical wink. "You assumed he was older, as everyone does." He was thoroughly entertained by this.

"Well, good. Finding rooms should be no problem then, assuming you can convince your friend to welcome some elves," Rainor said dryly.

"And maybe you can catch up on old times," Rachel added in a friendly tone, relieved that an old connection might help them out, at least until she had a chance to speak to her foster family.

They approached Brimley Downs at midday, ready for the comforts and amenities the town had to offer. Since the elves were not openly welcome in any part of Brimley, Eleese, Sage, Lea, Aryn and Rik opted to hide out at the old Patterson barn until Logan and Treyton could check out the inn. Rachel went with the others to the barn before making her way to the east toward the Mills'.

Rainor silently wondered if he should go with her, but when she straightened herself in the saddle and held her head high, he knew she was ready to tackle this on her own. He stayed with the other elves.

Logan and Treyton made their way through town to the tavern but decided to get some rooms secured first. They were welcomed at the front counter by a young lady with curly, blond hair and a crooked, yet sweet smile. Logan asked if she would have six rooms available and if Mathis was around.

She looked between the two brothers, past their shoulders, and said dryly, "You and your ghostly friends?"

Treyton spun around to look and the young lady laughed light-heartedly as she touched his arm to let him know she was only teasing them.

As they joined in her laughter, a broad-shouldered, bearded man came from a back room and boomed, "No rooms for scoundrels such as these!" causing the lady to retract her hand as she startled. Treyton's hand went to his sword hilt, but he sighed with relief when he saw his brother's smile.

"Mathis! So good to see you, *old* friend!"

"I see you've met my beautiful wife, Audelle." He wrapped one burly arm around her curvy frame and pulled her close. She giggled and leaned into him. "Did I hear you ask for six rooms? Who are you traveling with, and what are you up to for the need of so many?"

"Well ..." Logan began, "I might need a private word with you, if that is acceptable? I can answer you then."

"Sure, sure. Audelle, have the crew ready six rooms and some ale for these *boys*. We'll be in my office." He patted her rump as she stepped past him with a wink. "Come on back, fellas," Mathis directed the brothers to a comfortable office behind the front counter.

Treyton could hardly believe they were close in age. Mathis, indeed, seemed much older. The office had a stone fireplace with a mount above of a large, longhorn sheep and a bookshelf sparsely lined with tomes of various sizes.

Mathis sat behind a large, wooden desk in a high-backed, overstuffed, leather chair. He offered the brothers two wooden chairs opposite him. Shortly thereafter, Audelle entered with three large flasks of ale, and then excused herself, closing the door behind her.

Mathis sat with his hands folded on his desktop as he opened his mouth to question his longtime friend.

"Mathis, you've got a fine establishment and an even finer wife," Logan cut in with a wink. "This is my younger brother, Treyton. How do you feel about elves, old chum?" Logan didn't waste any time getting to the point.

Treyton's jaw clenched, and his eyes bulged. He took a deep swig of the ale in an effort to camouflage his surprise at his brother's bluntness. It was usually Treyton who had a way of blurting things out unexpectedly, not Logan.

Mathis leaned back in his chair with his hands bracing himself at the edges of the desk. He spluttered at the mention of the mostly taboo subject.

"That good, huh?" replied Logan as his gaze penetrated into Mathis' very soul.

"It's just that … well … hush your tone, friend. What you ask can get me into some serious trouble if the wrong ears are listening," he hissed in a low voice.

Logan leaned in and whispered again with a serious tone, "How do you feel about the elves?"

Mathis inhaled deeply, stroked his beard and ran his hand up and back down his broad face before releasing the air and responding. "I never met any of 'em … but I never understood what all the fuss was about," He leaned back momentarily, then sat back up to ask, "Why?" suddenly wondering where Logan stood on the issue.

"Not to worry. We just happen to be traveling with some. They've hidden themselves until I can secure rooms and their safety. Can you help us out?" Logan knew he could trust Mathis but didn't want to put him in an awkward position.

Mathis agreed to let them stay so long as they kept a low profile and didn't cause any trouble. Treyton and Logan assured Mathis there would be no trouble. They concluded their meeting, and the men paid handsomely for the rooms. As they left, Audelle promised the bathing rooms would be ready for the arrival of the rest of the group.

***

Rachel rode toward the home she had known most of her life. Her heartrate increased as she made her way past the Patterson farmland and Father Moore's farm. After the Bowman ranch, the Mills' farm would be to her right, just around the next corner. How long had she been away? All at once, it felt like too long. Her heart ached to see Jon, to tell him she brought help, to see him healed.

Can we really do it? Will Jack and Mavis allow Eleese to help? Will they even allow the group of elves in their home? She had to try.

Rachel spurred Chestnut into a trot as her anticipation swelled. She rounded the corner and nearly rode right into another horse galloping from the opposite direction.

"Rachel?" a familiar voice rang out in surprise. It was Lane. He wheeled his horse around to face her. "Rachel, you're back! You must get home at once, not a moment to waste. Jon has taken a turn for the worse. I was just leaving your parents' house to get Father Moore. I'll be back with him as soon as I can. GO!" Then he turned away and spurred his horse on again.

There was no time for pleasantries or the questions that had been burning in Lane's mind since the morning he found Rachel's note. He wanted to hold her in his arms and tell her how much he loved her, to comfort her through the certain loss of Jon, to tell her everything would be alright, but would it be? He rode to Father Moore's and wondered if Rachel still cared for him. Was she able to find help? Why was she alone? Was there still a chance that she would come back to him? Lane was not sure where they stood. There would be time for them to talk later. Now the only importance was placed on getting Father Moore and Rachel's ability to get to her little brother, even if only to say goodbye.

Rachel raced toward the house. In that short distance, between the corner and there, tears soaked Rachel's cheeks. Guilt flooded her heart over why she had left Jon. She wondered if it was partly her fault that his health had turned, if what Eleese had told her about the healing presence had kept him from the tipping point. She had to heal him now. She had to make things right. She may not have time to wait for Eleese's guidance.

She slid off Chestnut at the front of the house and hastily burst through the front door. She made her way back to the small room where she knew the boy would be sleeping. Mavis knelt by the bed, Jon's hand lay limp in hers as she cried softly. Jack slumped in a chair at the foot of the bed with his hand outstretched to lie on Jon's left ankle. They both looked up as Rachel entered the room. Fear now took the place of her adrenaline. Was she too late? Rachel gasped with relief when Jon's eyes opened slightly, and he turned to look up at her. He was so frail looking. There was little color in his hollow cheeks, and his normally bright eyes were dull and seemed unfocused.

"Oh Jon!" she sobbed, "I'm so sorry I left you," she knelt alongside Mavis and stroked Jon's hair gently across his forehead.

"Rachel?" Jack and Mavis chorused as they realized who had come in. Mavis stood and offered to make some tea. Lane entered with Father Moore just moments later, both panting.

"Lane, there's no time for me to explain, but I need a favor. Ride as fast as you can to the Patterson barn. Find Eleese. Tell her I need her, and bring her back here as quickly as you can. Use Chestnut if you need to." Rachel's eyes filled with tears yet again. Jack looked at her with concern, and Lane nodded once and was out the door. While Lane rode off to get Eleese, Father Moore prayed with Mavis in the kitchen. Rachel explained to Jack that she had gone in search of help and found it. She begged him to trust her and assured him she would explain everything once Jon was better. Mavis re-entered the room and set the tray of tea and cups down, only hearing part of what Rachel had said to Jack.

"He's dying, Rachel. We have tried everything," Mavis cried, tired and beyond consoling.

"You're upsetting your mother, Rachel. What help could you have possibly found that we have not already tried?" Jack half-scolded her as he embraced his wife.

Rachel was at a loss for words. She stood there with a pleading look in her eyes, as if to beg them not to give up. She sat on the edge of Jon's bed and held him. She held him tighter than she had ever held him before. His body was thin and felt cool. Her heart nearly burst with emotion.

Rachel's healing powers began to stir. Her body grew warm and began to tingle with the same hum her bracelet had made. She focused first on passing some of her warmth to Jon, remembering what Eleese had told her. The others in the room did not notice at first, but soon they could not ignore the rising temperature and the soft orange glow around their small child. Father Moore began to pray again. Rachel was trembling; she had not yet experienced a healing such as this. So far, she had only helped with wounds. Eleese had warned her that it would be different. She wasn't sure if she should stop or continue.

"What is happening? What are you doing to Jon?" Mavis wailed with concern, reaching for her child.

Jack, somehow sensing this was a good thing, held her back from snatching Jon away from Rachel. "Stay back, love. I think she is helping him," he soothed her.

Lane made it to the barn in record time and called out to Eleese as he approached, not sure where she would be or who he was looking for. "Eleese! Rachel needs you! Eleese! Please come quickly. It's Jon!"

Rainor was pacing the barn, able to feel his sister's emotions, as could Eleese. When they heard Lane, the two rushed out to greet him. He was obviously shocked to see an elf maiden before him, and possibly more shocked about the young man who stood with her.

"Where is she? Take us to her!" Eleese implored of him.

"I ... um ... yes ... well ..." Lane stammered briefly at the sight of Rainor before turning his horse, waves of jealousy threatening to surface. *Who is he? Why is* he *so concerned about Rachel?* A thought crossed Lane's mind that maybe *he* was Rachel's new love interest. If so, how could Lane compete? He mentally admonished himself for such petty thoughts at a time like this. There certainly were a great many questions for Lane to ask later.

Rainor mounted swiftly and reached down to lift Eleese to the back of his saddle. They galloped back toward the Mills' home. As they arrived in Jon's room, Jack and Mavis' mouths fell open at the sight of the petite elf that looked every bit like a sister to Rachel. Lane collapsed into a nearby chair. Rainor stood by the doorway staring intently toward Rachel. Eleese quickly sat at the other side of Jon's bed and held her daughter. The glow around them intensified. Jon's eyes opened, and he smiled at his parents.

"Oh!" Mavis squeaked as her hand covered her mouth, tears of joy now replacing the fear she had felt moments ago.

Eleese was quick to pick up on the fact that whatever illness this was, there was injury at a cellular level as well as infection. This would most likely take them some time to work through. The coating around Jon's spinal cord was scarred as well as some of the nerves in his brain. It was as if his cells were attacking each other. This affliction seemed to also be causing various parts of Jon's body to suffer and shut down.

The two focused on Jon's central nervous system initially then on to his heart, lungs, liver, and other internal organs. They repaired each tiny injury within before tackling the 'clean-up' as Eleese had referred to it earlier.

Two hours passed, Rachel strained and cried. Emotion surged through her healing touch. Eleese helped to guide her through the strenuous task of repairing Jon's frail body. Mavis' anguish melted away as color returned to Jon's face and he began to look around the room. Jack squeezed her tightly. Rachel and Eleese's eyes were both closed as they worked together to rid Jon's body of the disease that had tormented him.

Jack and Mavis paced alongside of where Lane still sat. Father Moore promised not to say a word of this to others as he quietly excused himself. The awe was written all over his face.

"Mama! It feels like tickles under my skin!" Jon suddenly blurted out with a vigorous laugh.

"Rachel, start to pull back," Eleese coached. "You're giving too much now."

Rachel was still trembling and sobbing from her efforts. She hadn't yet realized all that she had accomplished. Jon was going to be OK. She and Eleese had worked together to replace his depleted nervous system along with many other ailments the poor child had endured. Eleese had never seen such a disease. Rachel's eyes fluttered open, then she collapsed to the floor. Rainor was quick to step in and cradle her in his protective arms. Eleese reclined on the pillow next to Jon, exhausted.

"Are you magic?" Jon asked Eleese in awe, eyes wide, and then turned to Rainor. "Is Rachel alright?"

"I am an elf. Your sister and I have a touch of magic. Yes ... we healed you. But now we both must rest," she whispered to him as she took in a deep breath and yawned.

Mavis and Jack ran to Jon's side, hugging him and kissing him. Mavis gently grabbed his face in her hands and scanned every inch of him with wonderment. He had not looked this healthy even since before he had fallen ill. More tears streamed down her already soaked cheeks.

Jack offered Eleese some of the tea Mavis had brought in earlier and expressed his gratitude repeatedly. "You have saved him. You saved my boy! I cannot thank you enough!"

Jon got up and tested his leg strength. Carefully at first, he stepped around Rachel and Rainor, then did a little hop and a leap and soon was running out into the hall and back into the crowded little room. He was filled with laughter.

Rainor gently removed Rachel's boots and placed her carefully in the bed next to Eleese. It did not take Eleese long to fall into a tranquil slumber next to her daughter.

Mavis watched her son as he ran and jumped around the room. She also kept an eye on Rainor.

Rainor felt uncomfortable as now at least two pairs of eyes were on him. He could guess what they were wondering. It was obvious that somehow Rachel and Eleese were related ... but Rainor looked nothing like them. "Is there somewhere we could all sit and talk without disturbing Rachel and Eleese?"

Lane was holding his tongue, but his glare was hard to hide. Jon grabbed a hold of Rainor's hand, as if he had known him all his life and dragged him out of the room. He led him to the front sitting room then asked his mother if he could go outside. Jack was the last to leave the bedroom, closing the door as he followed the others. Mavis had hesitated with her answer to Jon's request, but Jack nodded and told her to let the boy enjoy some sun.

Jon was elated just to be able to be out of bed. He had nothing specific planned as he trotted out the door. What six-year-old would? He took in a deep breath and turned his face toward the sky. The sun warmed his cheeks. He had been in bed, unable to get up for nearly two full weeks since just shortly after Rachel had left. Jon stood in silence, eyes closed, arms outstretched to his sides, soaking up the rays. Slowly at first, but then picking up speed, he began to spin wildly. His laughter floated on the gentle afternoon breeze. He finally fell in a dizzy heap on the grass. He lay back and watched some clouds, trying to find a familiar shape.

Then he listened. He heard the occasional bug buzz past his head, the gentle rustle of leaves on a small tree Jack had recently planted, and the murmurs of the sheep in the pasture behind the house. Jon loved to visit the sheep. He quickly rose to his feet and ran back to see them. Looking at him now was certainly different than a day ago, even a few hours ago. He had been moments from knocking on death's door. And now, even at his young age, he was aware of how lucky he was to be alive. He would cherish every minute of his restored health.

Rainor, unsure of how much he should tell, without his sister awake to share the news herself, took in a few slow, deep breaths. "Let me first introduce myself. I am Rainor, son of Eleese, grandson of Chief Therek and Lin of Geerda." With his introduction he bowed regally. "Raiza, whom you know as Rachel, is my twin sister."

Mavis stared blankly at Rainor, shocked but with some recognition and understanding of all he had just announced. Jack scratched his head, trying to let the news sink in.

Lane sighed with relief and offered his hand in greeting, "I am Lane, Rachel's boyfriend ..." he began in a confident tone but it faded at the last word. Truly he was unsure of that status, now more than before as he met Rainor's eyes.

"She mentioned you," Rainor offered, but without additional explanation.

"I knew she was special, but not quite like this," Mavis said quietly. "Jack, if what this young man said is true, our Rachel and this young man are heirs to the throne ... you do realize what he has just told us, don't you?" she whispered to her husband with awe.

"We found and raised the lost Princess of Brimley?" Jack whispered in return.

Rainor was slightly confused. Lane was thoroughly confused.

Jack and Mavis turned to them and made them swear to secrecy. Jack began to explain.

"Rainor, I am guessing that you are aware of at least some of this information but possibly from a different point of view. Lane, this may all be new to you. When Desmond was our King, and Mavis and I were newlyweds, it was rumored that he had taken an elf for his bride, the chieftain's daughter – that would be Eleese. Am I right?" He looked to Rainor, who nodded in agreement. "And it was also rumored that they had a son – you?" Again he looked to Rainor who nodded again. "But when Stephan put Desmond in the dungeons, it is said that more than once he slipped and mentioned his 'children', not his 'child', and that he called out two names, presumably his son and daughter's names, after Stephan had beat him and left him for dead. Rumors have been hushed throughout the years to protect the possible lost daughter after we heard of the son's death. Obviously – you are not dead. You have no idea how many people have been holding onto hope, however slim it may be, that the true heir to the throne would somehow surface before it is too late!" As Jack spoke, he was entirely beside himself with exuberance.

Rainor could not believe what he was hearing. Not only did the elves hold out hope for him and his sister, but so did the humans – or at least for Rachel.

Lane was no longer confused, but he was still in shock. Rachel was royalty, no longer just the girl he loved from another farm.

***

Logan and Treyton had ridden back to the Patterson barn and Rik filled them in on what had transpired. The brothers wanted to ride to Rachel's side, but none of the group knew exactly where that was.

"Can't one of you summon her? Or Rainor? However you do that ... you know ... with your minds or whatever?" Treyton begged them frantically.

"No!" Aryn replied in a harsh tone. "We wait here. No further discussion."

Sage felt as the brothers did. He had grown quite fond of Rachel and truly thought of her as a sister. He was concerned for her and could not help but call out to Rainor for news. [*Brother, is there news? Can you share with us?*] he sent privately to Rainor.

[*Jon is well; Rachel and my mother are exhausted and sleeping. There's more, but now is not the time. I will come for the rest of you shortly,*] Rainor assured the group.

Guessing that Sage had prompted the communication, Aryn shot him a glare and shook his head. Sage could sense that Aryn was even more rigid than normal, but wasn't sure of the reason. The rest of the group shared with Logan and Treyton, and there was a moment of triumph at the news about Jon. Rachel and Eleese had been successful in their efforts.

Rainor told Jack and Mavis that he and Eleese had traveled with others and that he should go and tell them the news. Lane offered to go with him, but he declined, asking him to stay in case Rachel woke up. Rainor knew there was much for the two of them to discuss. Lane agreed and went out to check on Jon who was contentedly visiting with each of the sheep. Lane was astonished at how good he looked.

Mavis asked Rainor if they would all consider coming to the house later for a group supper. She wanted to meet the rest of their party and thank them all for helping Rachel. He assured her they would and let her know how many of them there were as he mounted his horse to leave.

Eleese was beginning to stir and recovered fairly quickly from her previous efforts. She arose from the bed and walked out to where she could hear Jack, Lane, and Mavis discussing the unbelievably good fortune of the day. They greeted her warmly as she entered the room. "Where is Rainor?"

"You just missed him; he left to share the news with the rest of your companions. I've offered for you all to dine with us tonight." Mavis looked at her with a hopeful expression.

"How much did Rainor share with you?" Eleese asked casually.

"Enough to know who you are and how you are related to our daughter ... to Rachel," Jack smiled with kindness to let Eleese know that the details were accepted.

"I know this is all a bit of a shock to you, and I am sorry that we weren't able to meet under different circumstances, but I want you to know my gratitude for the love and kindness you have all shown to my daughter. I thought I would never see her again, and it means a great deal to me that you have kept her safe and raised her as you have," Eleese spoke with the utmost sincerity.

Mavis had long wondered if the day would ever present itself that Rachel's real parents were revealed. She wondered if they had been killed or if they were alive somewhere. Now that the moment was actually staring her in the face, her reactions were different than she expected. She had always thought she would react in a defensive mode, ready to give them a piece of her mind about leaving their child alone in the bitterness of winter. She had imagined herself denying them access to their daughter, to the girl she and Jack had raised as their own. That feeling melted away in Eleese's presence. Mavis wanted to comfort her and make her feel welcome, wanted to encourage the relationship between mother and daughter. It made her heart swell when Eleese thanked them.

"I have no doubt that you would have done the same if the situation had been reversed," she told Eleese as she took her hands. "I have cared for your daughter, and you have healed my son. I know of no greater beginning to what I hope is a lifetime friendship." Mavis began to tear up again and wiped her tears away apologizing for her emotional state. She had had very little sleep in the past several days.

Rainor rode to the rest of the group at the Patterson barn and told them what had happened with Jon in more detail. He then explained what had come about with the Mills and the fact that it wasn't only the elves who were awaiting King Stephan's downfall. Everyone was relieved to hear that the Mills had accepted Rachel and Eleese's healing powers and seemed to be OK with harboring a group of elves as well. They decided to ride to the inn and get a bath before heading to dinner with Jack and Mavis. Logan and Treyton lead the way.

When they arrived at the inn, Audelle showed them to their rooms. Logan and Treyton would share a room, as well as Sage and Lea. Rik, Aryn, Eleese, and Rainor would each have a room to themselves. Once things were settled, Audelle showed them to the rooms that held the bathing tubs, one room for the men, one for the women. The rooms were large and open with one large, central tub at a cooler temperature, and several individual tubs around the edges of the room with fires underneath.

No one else was in the ladies bathing area, so Lea got her choice of tubs. A tall, slender, older woman came in to assist her. She had thin, grey hair pulled into a loose bun at the back of her head. She wore a long, simple, white gown that tied comfortably at the waist with the wide sleeves rolled up to her elbows. She handed Lea a large towel, some soap, and oils for her hair. She asked Lea if she wanted her clothing laundered and Lea agreed and thanked the woman. Before excusing herself, she told Lea to ring the bell if she was in need of anything further. Lea submerged into the tub. It felt wonderful to slip into the warm water and out of the sticky, dusty film from their travels.

The men weren't as lucky as Lea, and had to share the room with two others. There were just enough tubs for each of them but they could not speak freely amongst themselves. The other two men seemed to take no notice of the elves in the group, but Rik and Aryn remained wary of their presence. They were also given large towels and soaps and blades for shaving if they desired. Their clothes were taken for cleaning as well. It may not have been as private as they had hoped, but it was amazingly relaxing nonetheless.

Once everyone was bathed and dressed in some clean clothes, the group met up and went to the tavern next door to the inn. There was not much time before they would ride to the Mills' but a drink seemed in order. Rik, Aryn, Sage, and Lea followed Logan and Treyton as they scanned the room for any potential problems. The tavern was nearly empty. This was a good sign. The bar was to their left, a fifteen-foot long, smoothly polished plank of dark wood cut from a single tree. Stools were lined neatly at its edge. Several tables were arranged to their right. Directly ahead of them was an empty space, presumably for entertainers. They chose a table toward the far corner where they could see the rest of the room. A young man of about seventeen years came to ask what they would like. He appeared to be making a conscious effort not to let his gaze linger on Lea for too long. Sage gave him a playful snarl, and he fumbled backwards to get their drinks.

Rik, Logan, and Treyton decided on a stout brew that appeared rich and dark in their mugs. Sage and Rainor opted for a light ale with a nuttiness that lingered after drinking it. Lea chose mulled wine and Aryn had nothing, saying he preferred to arrive at the humans' home with a 'complete head'. The others merely stared at him a moment before going on with their conversations. Aryn ignored them.

Rachel did not want to wake up. She had a raging headache and was not completely certain where she was. Her eyes remained closed for a moment longer. She lay still, noting a familiarity in the scent of the room she was in. She could feel that she was in a bed covered by a soft quilt with no shoes on. She wiggled her toes. *At least they don't hurt.* Thoughts of the cottage in Brenton came to mind, and then they were suddenly chased away by thoughts of her home. She was home! She remembered the events of the day.

She rolled on her side and rubbed her eyes – no Jon, no Eleese, Mavis, Jack, Rainor, Lane – no one else was in the small room with her. She swung her legs down to the floor and noticed her boots placed neatly at the side of the bed. She slipped them on and stumbled into the hall. With one eye closed and her hand to her forehead, she fought back the bile that threatened to come up. Her body felt heavy. There was so much pain in her head.

Eleese turned first to greet her and touched her forehead gently with her slender fingers. The heaviness and pain melted away with Rachel's next few steps into the room. Rachel smiled sleepily at her then turned to greet her mother and father ... well, her Mavis and her Jack. *What will I call them now?*

They both smiled, and Jack pulled a chair around for her to join them. Lane looked at her with a new respect. He sat forward and handed her a cup of tea just how she liked it. He was a good man.

"Where is Rainor?" Rachel asked. "And Jon? Where are they?"

Jack pointed out the window that looked out to the west of the house. Jon was running with a few of the sheep and the Mills' farmhand. Rachel beamed at the sight of him out there.

"We did it, Mothe …" she cut the word short as her gaze went from Eleese to Mavis. She wasn't sure how much they knew.

"It's alright, Rachel. We know," Mavis smiled.

"Yes, you've been asleep for over two hours; did you think we would not have questions?" Jack teased.

"I had hoped that I would have more time to break the news to you gently, to ease into the facts of my lineage … at the very least," she replied with a shrug.

"Rainor went to join the others at the inn and get settled, but they should be here shortly for supper. Would you like a bath before they arrive?" Mavis asked as she looked from Rachel to Eleese, as she offered them at least a wash basin of warm water to freshen up. There wouldn't be time for two to bathe properly. The wash basin was perfectly acceptable to both of them, but Eleese told Rachel to go ahead and take the bath.

With two mothers looking on, she wasn't about to argue. Rachel was eager to remove the less than pristine riding clothes and don her favorite dress from her own closet. She had not moved all of her items to Lane's. She was suddenly glad of this fact. Mavis went about drawing the bath for Rachel and brought Eleese to the other room to freshen up.

While Rachel waited, Lane watched her intently. "May I have a moment alone with your daughter?" he directed his question to Jack.

"She is no longer bound by my wishes. It is completely up to her." He gave her hand a gentle squeeze.

"That will be fine, although I am sure we will need more time than what we have at the present. It will be a good start." She wasn't sure where to begin with Lane. The way he looked at her was filled with longing. It nearly broke her heart. She was angry with herself for giving him false hope that she would somehow get to the same place he was with his feelings. She knew now that was not the case. There would always be a soft spot in her heart for him, but she wouldn't love him the way he wanted.

Jack excused himself from the room to head outside with Jon. Lane stood to embrace Rachel. It felt awkward, and she pulled away and sat down. He sat across from her, leaning forward with his elbows on his knees.

"There are some things I need to tell you, Lane," she started. "I am a different person now with a different path to follow. I have quite a burden to take on with Rainor, and I am not sure how you will fit into my future. I know you have questioned our relationship. I have as well. I don't love you the way you love me, and I'm sorry if that hurts you. I truly am." She stared down at her fingers as she fiddled with the end of her braid. She couldn't bear to see the hurt look on Lane's face. She was proud of herself for getting everything out though.

"Rachel, you know I love you. I can wait for you. I can be by your side and help you get through the next phase of your life … if you'll just give me that chance," he pleaded with her.

She sighed. It almost would have been easier if he had gotten angry and stormed out, but he didn't. He stayed to beg, "Just tell me what you need from me, Rachel."

"I need you to let me go, Lane." She met his gaze briefly then let her shoulders and her eyes drop once more. She knew she was hurting him, but it was the right thing to do.

"No," he said simply, as if there was nothing more to discuss. He rose from the chair and paced the room. "If it is because of the throne, let your brother have it. You know nothing of being a ruler. You only know this life. Marry me and we will *make* it work. We will." He just didn't seem to understand. Rachel didn't have the same feelings for him that he had for her.

"Lane ... I cannot marry you. You deserve the love of someone who will return your feelings. I'm not that person. I guess I have known it for some time. I can't keep giving you hope that isn't there. It's not fair. You've been a wonderful friend to me."

"FRIEND?" Lane cut her off. Here comes the anger. "A friend ... I see ..." his voice lowered to a growl, "I will stay for dinner because your mother asked me to. Then I will leave. You may come for your things tomorrow," he stormed out of the house with his hands running through his hair in frustration.

Mavis re-entered the room to take Rachel to her bath. She had heard most of the conversation. "Oh, Rachel. He will get over this, but it will take some time. He had hoped that you would come back ready to commit yourself to him; he has been visiting nearly every day. He asked your father's permission for your hand ... but I suspect he already knew the truth. Hearing it out loud just hurts a little more." She swept the loose hairs from Rachel's braid across her forehead then set her hands to Rachel's shoulders. "Come, let's get you cleaned up."

It was a quick bath, but nothing less than invigorating. She went to her old room afterwards and found the dress she would wear. It was her favorite for wearing when the Mills had company. It was a deep blue, soft material, which moved with Rachel. The neckline was just low enough to be slightly flirtatious. The bodice and sleeves were fitted to her slender frame. There was a touch of lace trimming at the neckline, sleeves, and hem. It felt loose since the last time she wore it; she must have lost some weight on her journey. It was still comfortable and gave her a feeling of confidence. She asked Mavis if she would braid her hair in a style that swept across her brow, over one ear, then wrapped around the nape of her neck to the opposite side, allowing the remaining hair to curl gently down her shoulder.

"Stunning," Eleese said as she entered the room. "I know of at least four young men who won't be able to ignore your beauty tonight," she said with brows raised.

"Oh, no. You know that is *not* my intention! Wait ... which ones?" Rachel's brows pinched together and her head tilted as she turned to Eleese for an answer.

"Come, now. Isn't it obvious? Lane, for one ... Logan, Treyton, and Aryn," she held up a finger as she named off each of them.

"Aryn?" Rachel blurted out and then quickly added the other names. Eleese just laughed softly, as did Mavis.

After Lane's exit, it was only a short time before he had cooled off and joined Jack and Jon in the pasture. He was not normally quick to temper.

"It's nothing shy of a miracle. Look at him!" Jack said as Lane approached. The two men stood, leaning on the fence, watching Jon as he played. Never-ending energy seemed to ooze from the child now. "Why so down, Lane?" Jack turned to ponder the sour expression Lane couldn't hide if he tried.

"Rachel," was all he said.

"Hmm," Jack replied. He wasn't sure exactly what had transpired, but it was fairly obvious things had changed since Rachel left. They stood in silence for a moment. The crunch of several hooves on the gravel path up to the house broke the silence. "That will be tonight's guests. Let's put on a happy face and make them feel welcome, shall we?" Jack clapped his hand on Lane's shoulder and called to

Jon to come inside, gave a wave to the farmhand and turned toward the house.

Eleese and Mavis met the group out front as Rachel finished getting her shoes on. Rik was the first to introduce himself to Mavis and continued to introduce the rest as well. Jack, Lane, and Jon came over just as the guests made their way toward the

door and the introductions were repeated. They were met warmly and welcomed into the home.

Lane was in no mood to be social but put on a 'happy face' as Jack had asked. No one, save Rainor, sensed anything of his true mood. After Logan and Treyton were introduced to Lane, Treyton turned and whispered to his brother, "What is Lane doing here?"

Logan replied just as quietly, "Promise me you'll be pleasant."

Mavis was about to leave the room to get drinks for everyone when Rachel stepped in. She smiled brightly at everyone. As the men stood to greet her, Mavis noticed the truth to Eleese's earlier comment about the four in particular. She noticed a sudden sadness in Lane's eyes but a spark in the eyes of the others. Rachel had to have sensed it as well, at least to some extent, and blushed from the attention.

"You look beautiful this evening," Rainor offered with a smile.

"Thank you. You all cleaned up nicely as well," as she motioned around the room. Jon ran over to give her a hug. He hadn't seen her since she had healed him.

[*Good job,*] The words tickled her mind like a feather at the cusp of consciousness. She didn't have long to wonder who had spoken them when her thoughts were suddenly brought back to Jon.

"Rachel, you made me better! I don't know how, but you did! And I missed you!"

She leaned down to hug him back then turned him around to ask if everyone had met him. She was so happy to see him looking so alive. "I missed you too, Jon. I'll tell you all about my adventures while we eat!"

"It's been a long time since we had such a large crew for supper. We had to let some of the help go because of the recent medical costs, but the remaining kitchen staff have outdone themselves tonight!" Jack announced as they seated themselves at the large dining table.

The feast consisted of two roasted chickens, boiled potatoes with herbs, caramelized carrots, and warm rolls with preserves. Rachel relayed most of the events of her journey up until meeting Rainor.

The rest of the group joined in as they narrated their involvement. Some topics were left unsaid, like Rachel's troubles in Brenton or Lea's ability to shape-shift, but otherwise the events played out as Jon sat wide-eyed in amazement. Jack, Mavis, and even Lane bounced questions off the rest of the group. Jon requested a retelling of the encounter with the jackoyts, much to Mavis' dismay. She cringed at the horror of its retelling, but allowed it.

After the stress was gone from almost losing Jon and not having a clue where Rachel had been the last couple of weeks, Mavis was in fine spirits. Now she allowed herself to relax and enjoy the company. She had consumed her share of wine and was rather enjoying the evening. She was a very observant woman, quick to notice the continued glances from Lane to Rachel, from Logan to Rachel, from Treyton to Rachel, and even a few (though he hid them well) from Aryn to Rachel. *Eleese had been spot-on. Was*

Rachel oblivious to the attention of these handsome young men?

Jack was always a handsome man in Mavis' eyes, but not a highly sought-after man, even in his younger years. Lane was not bad looking either, but these other men … *Goodness.* She concluded that with Rik and the younger men, there may have been seven of the most handsome men she had ever laid eyes on at her dining table. Half of the men present were pining over Rachel. "Oh … to be young again," Mavis said under her breath as she took another glass of wine. Jack was relieved to see his wife able to relax. It had been too long since she had looked so content. He smiled at her.

As the meal came to an end, Rachel scanned the friends and family seated with her. Sage and Lea sat close together, talking quietly with Eleese, fingers of one hand lovingly intertwined. Rik and Logan were in conversation with Jack and Lane about possible plans to rally the town against Stephan. Treyton and Rainor were entertaining Jon and Mavis with riddles. Rachel's gaze finally fell upon Aryn. He was staring at her; the faintest of smiles graced his lips. He sat very still, with his hands folded in front of him. She realized he was the only other person at the table not engaged in conversation.

[*Happy?*] It was such a simple question; the thought was quiet and soft in her mind, not unlike the other messages she had received that were still a bit mysterious. Just the feeling of the word seemed to caress her thoughts. Her eyes darted to Rainor – it wasn't from him – then to Rik, and Sage. It wasn't Rik or Sage; they were too engaged in their own conversations. That left one other possibility. It had to be Aryn, his hazel eyes still locked onto her.

Rachel's heart fluttered at the realization that Aryn was speaking to her in such an intimate manner. [*Yes, very,*] she replied back with one side of her lip curling into a shy smile. When Aryn returned the gesture, Rachel nearly melted into a puddle. She looked away and tried to steady her breathing. What was that all about? Better yet, why did that simple question feel like such a big deal? She hoped he was not toying with her.

Rainor turned toward her with a broad grin plastered on his face. He could feel her joy. All was as it should be, at least for now.

The evening came to a close with Lane thanking Jack and Mavis for the dinner and giving Jon a hug. As he left for his home, he asked Rachel if she would still be coming to see him the following day for her things. She told him she would. When she offered to walk him to the door, he declined. Giving a solemn nod, he showed himself out.

Sage and Lea tried to hide the fact that they were eager to get back to the privacy of their room at the inn, but most everyone understood. Eleese was ready for a good night's rest in something other than a tent so she encouraged the others to bid their farewells.

Rainor gave his sister a long embrace. [*Your efforts were worthwhile. Get some rest, and tomorrow your future begins,*] he reminded her.

Rachel would stay with the Mills' tonight. The others offered their thanks and stepped out into the warm evening air. Rachel wasn't ready to think of the future just yet, so she focused on the moment. Her journey had come to an end.

Jarrell's Vision
The Throne of Brimley Series
Book 2

Rachel's Journey had taken her from her home in Brimley Downs to the elven village of Geerda and back home again to ultimately save Jon's life.

Now she has a new life to look forward to, and more questions to be answered. Will they ever find out what happened to her original foster family? How will she and her new-found friends and family right the wrongs of her second cousin? Will she and her brother be accepted by humanity as the rightful King and Queen of Brimley?

Continue reading Rachel's story in book two of The Throne of Brimley: Jarrell's Vision.

ABOUT THE AUTHOR

Merri Gammage is a creative and passionate author who wants to share her imagination with others. She has years of ideas ready to be written and presented to her readers.

Raised in the Pacific Northwest, she was surrounded with a visual array of landscapes from beaches to mountain peaks and everything in between. Her stories stem from a fascination with mythical creatures, exploring evergreen forests, combing the beach for oddities, and daydreaming on misty mornings – a perfect backdrop for adventure, fairy tales, and whimsy. Creating makes Merri happy. Her theory is that everyone deserves an occasional get-away, an escape into the imagination.

When Merri isn't writing or working, she enjoys reading and spending time with her husband and their grown children. They have an older son and a younger set of twins (one boy, one girl). In the summer months, the family enjoys camping and the outdoors. They also find great fulfillment in giving back to their community. All five of them are involved with their local fire department: one full-time Firefighter/EMT, two part-time Firefighters, and two Associate Members (who assist the firefighters on scene, with training and fundraisers).

Merri plans to continue reading, writing, sharing her ideas with others, and living life to the fullest.

50300178R10160

Made in the USA
Lexington, KY
27 August 2019